T0208868

Lillian
(A SEQUEL TO BOBBY)

JEAN McDOWELL

WESTBOW
PRESS®
A DIVISION OF THOMAS NELSON
& ZONDERVAN

WestBow Press books may be ordered through booksellers or by contacting:

WestBow Press
A Division of Thomas Nelson & Zondervan
1663 Liberty Drive
Bloomington, IN 47403
www.westbowpress.com
844-714-3454

Scripture taken from the King James Version of the Bible.

ISBN: 978-1-6642-7136-4 (sc)
ISBN: 978-1-6642-7135-7 (hc)
ISBN: 978-1-6642-7137-1 (e)

Library of Congress Control Number: 2022912341

Print information available on the last page.

WestBow Press rev. date: 08/05/2022

Chapter 1

MY NAME IS LILLIAN SWANSON. WHEN I WAS BORN, I had three brothers. I never heard my parents call each other by their first names, and I did not think to ask. He was Sir and my mother was Mom. My brothers were Joseph, Thomas, and Robert. Our home was strange. My mother was sometimes a loving person and did everything she could to make us feel loved during the day. In the evenings when my father was there, it was like a different place because everything changed. The atmosphere was different, my mother was different, and my brothers were different. It took me a while to catch on that no one was supposed to speak in the evening unless my father spoke to him or her. When I was born, my oldest brother was five years-old. It must have been difficult for my mother to have four children five years-old and younger, especially when she could not give them any attention after 6:00 p.m. She more or less ignored us when my father was home because he demanded all her attention. As I grew older, I thought he treated her more like a slave than a wife. I have always found it difficult to have friendships with boys or men and I am sure my early life experiences have a lot to do with that.

My father always seemed to be angry and my mother always seemed to be apologizing to him. For a long time, I wished she would stop doing the things which upset him. Later I realized no matter what she did, he was never happy. He became angry easily and no one knew what might set him off. As far back as I can remember, when my father became violent, Joseph would take Robert and me to his bedroom and tell us stories. We spent many long hours sitting on his bed. When I think back, I realize how skillful he was for a six-year-old. Thomas, the four-year-old, was more than Joseph could handle, so Thomas would stand at Mother's knee. Although my father would not pay attention to him, Joseph knew he needed to be quiet, so he would stand there and hear all the verbal abuse my father would give to my mother.

My father would rant and rave from the moment he came through the door until he went to bed. My mother could not come and say goodnight because it would have invoked his wrath and she lived in fear of him. He yelled and screamed at her every night. When I grew older, I realized he also beat her. She managed to keep this hidden from us when we were small because we were in our rooms and she retreated to her bedroom before the violence started. In the mornings when we awakened, we always waited for her to tell us to come for breakfast. That way we did not have to see our father in the morning. My mother often had bruises on her face and arms and, when one of us would pass remarks, she would say she was clumsy and had bumped into something. Later on, I figured out that my father had beaten her.

Sometimes I hated my mother because she didn't stand up to him, and at other times I wished she would take us all somewhere else where my father would not find us. He never hit me, but I think that was probably because of my mother's skillful manipulation of the battlefield. She almost never allowed herself to be beaten in the living room; she always managed to draw my father away from there when she knew a beating was coming. By doing that, none of her children ever saw any of the beatings. I will never know why she did that although I suspect it was to prevent any of us from reporting our father or to prevent any of us from getting involved in the violence.

My mother was a good cook, but my father was never pleased with anything she made. We would eat our meal in silence and, at the first opportunity, we would go to our bedrooms. I slept in a room by myself until I was seven or eight years old. I suffered from night terrors, and I would climb into bed beside Robert because he was the only one who would wake up. He would hold me until I stopped shaking and fell asleep. I always woke up in my own bed every morning and never really thought about how I got there until years later.

I remember a few times my father would take off for a week at a time and we would not know where he was. My mother seemed more agitated at these times and now I know it was because each time he came back, he was more violent than before. We loved it when he was gone. We talked aloud. Everybody talked and my mother was able to listen to our stories of school and play. I heard her laugh on those occasions, and it sounded strange.

When I was eight, a new baby, Ruth, arrived. She was beautiful; she cooed and giggled and made me happy. She slept in my room and even though I had to get up at night to feed and change her, I did not care because I was no longer alone. The first night after my mother brought her home from the hospital, she left Ruth in my room sleeping in a drawer on the floor. Mother asked me to feed her through the night and showed me where her bottles were. I more or less became her caregiver from six in the evening until my father left for work in the morning. My mother prepared her bottles and left them by Ruth's little makeshift bed. Each morning she thanked me, hugged me, and begged me to keep Ruth quiet the following night. I loved that child more than I loved anyone else because she was really my baby until I was at school. I missed her when I went to school and wished I could stay home.

I mentioned this to my mother one morning and she told me it was important I went to school because it was my ticket to a different life. I pondered that remark for a long time, not really understanding what it meant. I wondered why she had chosen this life if she didn't like it. I decided I would never get married and certainly never have children of my own. I loved school so it was not difficult for my mother to persuade me that I needed to continue to go there. School was wonderful because we could go to the library and read whatever books we wanted. Sometimes we brought them home to finish, but my father would scream about wasting money on stupid books. My mother asked us to keep all our books in our rooms so they did not come to his attention. We had no toys or games. We had no music. Life in our home was mainly about keeping out of our father's way. Sometimes I imagine I see him in the street or in a store and I tremble. I hate myself for that because I know he still has control over me, but I have neither seen him nor heard from him in years.

Ruth was a happy child, or seemed to be most of the time, but when my father was home she trembled and I would stay close to her. I remember when she started school; she was scared to leave our mother. Robert, as usual, took over and was able to calm her. When we reached her school, he went in with her and stayed until she was willing to stay with her teacher. Robert, the youngest of my brothers, is the one I miss most He was always there if I needed someone. He walked to school with me and always looked for me so we could walk home together. I treated him badly when I last saw him and he will probably never talk to me again, even if we meet. He and I would talk to each other on the way to and from school. When Ruth was with us, she skipped in front of us so we could talk freely without her hearing our conversation. Bobby, as we called him when our father was not around, tried to see the better side of everything. When I complained about Mother, he would tell me that she was doing the best she could. He did not like the situation any more than I did but he seemed more able to accept it.

I became more resentful as I grew older. I hated that my mother prayed; it was ridiculous to me to pray to God. I knew if there was a god, he would not allow anyone to live in our situation. Bobby would tell me Mother was probably praying because there was nothing else she could do. Sometimes I thought she was a stupid coward, and I would tell Bobby. He did not want to hear such things and always stood up for her, so I would drop the subject.

When I was fourteen, a girl from my grade asked if she could walk with us to Ruthie's school. Anna was her name and she started walking with us after school as well. Her little brother had started going to Ruthie's school. Anna was not in my class but I had seen her around the school. Bobby started talking to her more than he talked to me and I was jealous. I decided I did not like her and it irritated me that Ruthie showed clearly that she did. She was a sweet person but because she was my age I thought she should talk to me more than she talked to Bobby. Now I know it was probably because I was always complaining. At home sometimes I would hear Bobby saying her name repeatedly, as if he liked the sound of it. I thought he was stupid. I had reached the point where I resented Ruthie also. She was such a pest, always wanting me to hold her and always trembling. I wished she would grow up. Mostly she went to Bobby for comfort.

One day Bobby, who had started working in a store nearby, came home very excited. Anna's father came to the store where Bobby worked and invited our whole family for a Fourth of July celebration. There was to be a barbecue and fireworks. It sounded wonderful and Bobby tried to persuade my mother to go. She was her usual scared self and said she could not go but we could go. I was ecstatic. We had never gone anywhere; even school trips were a no-no because we had to be home before our dad. My mother said if our dad was working the next day, we could go and, as he usually worked on holidays, it would probably work out. She said she would bake some pies and we could take them. For once, I was thankful for my mother, only because she made the best pies. Taking them would make me feel important, so I hugged her and asked her if she would make apple. I remember she responded with her own hug and told me she loved me. It made me feel warm and fuzzy inside. I knew that even though she did not always do the things I wanted her to do, she loved me and I loved her. That tender moment has stayed very clear in my head and heart.

That evening was awful. My dad came home from work in a foul mood. He shouted, cursed, and threw things around for hours after supper. I sat in my room alone listening to the unspeakable things he said to my mother and for the first time I realized I felt sorry for her and did not hate her. I was full of loathing for my father and decided I would do everything in my power to get her away from him. I also prayed God would do something to end all this misery. It was strange because I was not at all sure there was a God but I prayed anyway. I thought maybe if I prayed with my mother God would know there was something wrong. I had heard my mother's prayers and I knew she never mentioned my dad in her prayers. She simply asked God to keep us safe. She named each one of us and was particularly tearful when she spoke of Joseph and Thomas. Both of them had left after Thomas tried to intervene in one of Dad's tirades and been locked out of the house by my father. They had taken off the next day and we had not seen them since.

My mother always came to our rooms in the morning to tell us breakfast was ready and our father had left. That Fourth of July morning we waited and waited but she did not come. After waiting for a long time Bobby told us he would make some breakfast. He said Mom must be tired and he was going to let her sleep. We cleaned up the dishes and willed her awake; she had pies to bake and I hoped she would change her mind and come with us after all. Later that morning, she came out of her bedroom and I had to turn my face away. She looked hideous. Her face was black and blue; one eye was swollen and closed. We all gasped. Bobby jumped up and asked her if she needed to see a doctor but she told him it was all right. She had to hold on to him as he guided her to the couch. She said that she would lie down again for a while and she would bake the pies later. She fell asleep and as time passed, I began to feel resentful again. We were supposed to leave at noon, the pies needed to bake, and I knew there would be no pies and no glory for me. I was so selfish; all I wanted was to look good to others and thoughts of having no pies to take filled my mind more than my mother's condition.

Bobby decided we would not wake her up and when I complained about having no pies, he said he had some money saved and we would leave early to buy fruit at the fruit stand. When it was nearly noon, we left to do the shopping. I remember Bobby going over to kiss my mom. I was mad at her for not making the pies so I did not feel like kissing her. I did have a pang of guilt when Ruthie asked Bobby where she should put her kiss so it would not hurt Mother's face. I almost changed my mind but did not, and I have regretted that decision ever since.

Chapter 2

W E HAD A WONDERFUL DAY AT ANNA'S HOME. SHE turned out to like me as much as much as Bobby; in fact she spent most of the day with Ruthie and me. She even found swimsuits for us and we splashed all day in their pool. It was so different from our home. I felt at times that I was dreaming. Her dad and brother played ball with Bobby, a couple of other men, and two boys from school. Anna was nice to me and gave my sister and me so much attention that I chided myself for thinking she liked Bobby more than she liked me. Everyone was happy there. Anna's mom was always smiling, and I thought of my own mom with her bruised face and felt remorse about my resentment. Bobby decided that we should go home around four to see if our mother would come. I did not want to go, but he said he had made arrangements for a place for us all to stay and we needed to go pack our clothes and get Mom. I was so excited I walked so fast I almost ran—until we saw our dad's truck in the driveway. I thought I was going to vomit. We kept hurrying and I could see that Bobby was distraught.

After we went inside, things got weird. My dad was packing a bag. My mom was still asleep. My dad grabbed Ruthie and put her in the truck, and then he tried to pull me in as well. I resisted and with Bobby's help got away. I was so scared. Bobby lifted a screaming Ruthie out of the front seat and carried her back into the house. My dad was so mad I thought he would kill us all. Then suddenly, he grabbed his bag and was gone. He screeched out of the driveway and tore out a shrub at the corner because he was in such a hurry. At least we could get Mom and go. Bobby went to wake Mom. He turned white and ran to a neighbor to have them call an ambulance. I did not know then that my mother was dead from the injuries inflicted by my dad. Soon the paramedics arrived and then the police, who were quite mean to Bobby. I was scared and Ruthie was trembling again. I wished my dad were dead; I would have killed him myself at that moment. My mother was dead and I had been mad at her for not making pies. I had not even kissed her goodbye. Now she was dead and gone forever.

My mind was in such turmoil. I was unable to think straight. I was unaware of what was really happening until a couple of hours later. Bobby, Ruthie, and I were taken in a car to a large building and Ruthie and I were taken to a long hallway. The social worker opened a door and told me to go inside the room. I was left alone in that room without explanation of any kind. I was so tired I just sat on the bed, numb. Bobby appeared and told me to wait until all was quiet and then go next door to get Ruthie or stay with her in her room. He said she was right next door, and they were taking him to another part of the building but Ruthie was not allowed in the same room with him. He knew Ruthie would be terrified so he asked me to do this for him. He was very emotional and I agreed to do as he asked. Then he joined the social worker who had been in Ruthie's room and walked away. I waited for a few minutes after Bobby and the social worker left and then I went into the room next door. I felt so sorry for my little sister and knew she understood less than me about what was going on. I held Ruthie until she fell asleep, then I climbed into bed beside her and fell into a troubled sleep full of chaos and bad dreams.

The following morning I was awake before the social worker came. She brought Ruthie and me to a large office where we waited, holding each other's hands, until a nice woman took Ruthie's hand and led her away. Ruthie walked slowly looking at me with fear in her eyes. We never even said goodbye and I never saw her again. I was taken along a hallway to another room and there I stayed for an hour or two reading magazines. Then a man and woman came in with a girl who was about my age. I had seen her in school but did not know her name. They took me home and told me they were my new foster parents. I had my own room and it was nice. I asked about Ruthie but they did not know anything. I was torn between worrying about my sister and really liking my new home. I made myself believe that

Bobby had abandoned us, that Ruthie was in a home like this too, and that I should just enjoy my new home. I had a fleeting thought that this was God's answer to my prayer, but it was fleeting and I never thought too much about God for a long time after that.

My new parents were kind, not loving like my mom but kind and generous. They had my hair cut and styled the same as their daughter; they bought me new clothes. I was able to go back to school and be with the popular girls. I liked that. One day I saw Bobby and he nearly squeezed the breath out of me. I was somewhat embarrassed and when he started telling me he had plans to get Ruthie and me together and go live somewhere, I told him I had to go to class. I felt bad but I did not want to give up my new life. He looked so hurt I almost went after him, then changed my mind and ran after my friends. Every time I saw him after that, I would go in the opposite direction. One day he cornered me and told me he missed me and wanted to talk to me. I told him to get lost because I had new friends and a new home and did not want to be reminded of my former one. I turned and walked away from him. I knew he did not deserve that because he had always done what was best for me, but I did not want my present situation to change. He shouted after me that he would always love me. I did not even turn around or acknowledge him. I never saw him again either.

My life was good as far as material things went. My foster sister Helen and I got on very well, possibly because I did everything she wanted although sometimes I felt mean saying and doing what she thought was fun. She encouraged me to ignore certain kids or be mean to them. She made fun of those who were not in her circle and encouraged me to do the same. She would invite certain girls to our home to hang out. She was careful to ask only those who had homes as big as ours. It was so different and I remember being ignored and having twangs of conscience. I was not bothered long and would soon help plan what we would do the following day and who was the next person to be humiliated. For the most part I liked my life and was relatively happy. There were times when I thought of my sweet Mom and wondered what she would think of my new life and family. At home, Helen would brag about who her friends were and ridicule those girls who did not have clothes as nice as ours. I would agree with her even though I knew she was just being mean. Our home was large with a pool and a tennis court. My room was identical to Helen's room. My foster parents bought two of everything so we would both have the same things. I had nice clothes, we shopped in the best stores, and I had all I could possibly want or need, yet there was an emptiness I could not quite fill. I did not allow myself to dwell on this because I was afraid that if I did, things would change, and I did not want that to happen. I resolved to put those thoughts as far back in my mind as I could and be content with what I had.

One Christmas we went to a large, ornate church with lots of statues around the walls. We sang songs from a book and the words tickled my memories about my Mom and God. I remembered my mother's prayers when the priest stood up at the front and read a prayer to God. It sounded so rehearsed compared to my mother's pleas for the safety of her children. He also read from a book called the Bible. I thought about God for a long time after that but kept my thoughts to myself. I was in the library in school and saw several versions of the Bible. One was called the King James Version. I thought if a king liked it then I would like it too. I brought it home and kept it in my room. I decided to keep my interest in that book from Helen and her parents. I read about how God created the world and saw that everything was good. I wondered how he could ever think that the home I had been born into could ever be thought of as good. I was not able to read much before the book was due back, so I decided to buy a copy for myself. It took a few months before I was able to do so but when I got it, I secreted it in a drawer in my bedside table. I read it sometimes when I was alone and I was amazed at the things which were written there. Some of it was boring and difficult to understand and after a couple of months, my interest in it waned and there it sat hidden under booklets and things in my drawer.

The summer before my senior year was momentous. We traveled to France, visited the Eiffel Tower, and toured villages. The people there were friendly and tried to speak English to us. The food was so delicious I thought I might one day be a chef. I had started thinking about college, which was the accepted thing to do after high school, but I couldn't make up my mind what I wanted to study. We had many conversations about our options when we ate our evening meal together. That was one thing I enjoyed. Memories of my former life and the meals I had eaten there in silence flooded my mind occasionally. The week before school started my foster mother made appointments for Helen and me at a clinic. The doctor examined me from head to toe. I was so embarrassed. The doctor and nurse asked me if I had ever had sex. I told them I never would and the nurse laughed at me. They prescribed a medicine for me and told me to be sure to take it every day at the same time. I asked them what it was for and was told it would keep me safe. On the way home, Helen told me she had the same medicine and it was to prevent pregnancy. I thought long and hard about that because I did not ever want to be pregnant. Being pregnant resulted in babies and babies had fathers and I was never going to be in that situation. I thought about my future and what my plans were and realized I had none.

Senior year was much different than other years at school. There were more free periods and lots of fun. Helen and I were invited to parties every week. We were allowed to go even if it was a school night. That meant sleeping late and missing the first class sometimes. My foster parents' solution to that was to buy a car for Helen so she could drive us to school. Sometimes the parties were not much fun because some of the kids would be drunk and would remind me of my dad. I saw how alcohol changed their personalities and decided it was not for me. I noticed that Helen drank quite a bit and would have me drive us home. I liked that; it made me feel rich. I also noticed that Helen would often disappear into a bedroom at a party and come out with her hair mussed. I was pretty sure what she was doing in there and asked her on the way home one night if she was not worried about being pregnant. She laughed and said that was the reason for the medicine we were taking. She said I should not be worried either. Of course I wasn't worried because I had no intention of having sex with any guy, so I didn't bother telling her I was not taking the medicine my foster mother gave me.

Helen and I were making plans for college, and were waiting for the acceptance letters with all the details of costs and accommodations. I assumed my foster parents were going to pay for my college fees. They always talked about Helen and I doing this and that together and I never thought too much about money or costs. There always seemed to be plenty of money to go around. We had applied to all the best universities and received numerous packages, all of which needed to be read, filled out, and mailed back. It was quite a chore but we had started early so we took our time.

We were at a party one night just before Christmas, and we were dancing and having a great time. This new boy, tall and blond, asked me to dance. I think my heart missed a beat. I thought for the first time ever that I might actually like a guy. He was sweet and gentle and asked me if I was having a good time. I told him I was and we danced for quite a while. I was getting tired so he suggested going to the front porch to chat. It was quieter out there and we chatted for a while. After a few minutes he asked me if I would like something to drink. I told him I would like some water. He looked surprised and asked if I was sure. I told him I didn't drink alcohol and he brought me water. He had a beer but was not drunk so I felt comfortable with him. That's all I remember about that night except for a few hazy recollections of being carried and waking up to see Helen grinning at me. I was not sure what had happened but I tried to put it out of my mind and concentrate on college papers and school classes. I had difficulty doing this and Helen was irritated with me more than once.

Chapter 3

*J*ANUARY CAME AND WE HAD SNOW. I LOVED HOW snow made everything look so crisp and clean. We went skiing every weekend. February started out the same way, but halfway through the month I woke up feeling ill. It was a Friday and our parents had informed the school that we were vacationing for the next six days. Usually I loved the sport but I didn't feel like going skiing. When the family went away for a long weekend, I stayed home and tried to finish my applications. I woke up every morning feeling ill but by the afternoon I was all right. When the family came home around suppertime on Wednesday, my foster mother asked me how I was and I told her I was fine. Next morning I felt ill again and she made an appointment for me to see the doctor. The doctor asked me a few questions and then did some tests. She came in to tell me the results of the tests and asked me if I had been taking the medicine she prescribed. I told her I had not because I didn't need it as I was not having sex. She then said the words that made my head spin: "You are pregnant, young lady."

"I can't be. I've never had sex!" How could this be? The doctor had obviously mixed my test up with some other person's and I told her so. She put her arm around me and said she realized it was a shock but there was no mistake. The test was positive. I was in turmoil. The doctor was talking but I couldn't concentrate. How did this happen? I realized the doctor was telling me things I needed to know and I tried to listen. I started to weep and tell the doctor that I had never had sex and didn't understand how this could be. She patiently asked me if I had a boyfriend. I told her I didn't. She asked me who I had been with just before Christmas. I told her again that I had never had sex. She asked me if I drank a lot of alcohol and I told her I didn't drink it at all. I told her I had been to a party just before Christmas and had water to drink. Then I remembered the strangeness of that night and told her about it. She took some papers from her desk and started filling them out. She said she would tell my foster mother and I should go home to wait for her. Helen had dropped me off so I called her to come get me and told her I was pregnant. She was horrified and asked me if I had forgotten my pill. I told her I had not been taking them and she told me I was stupid. She dropped me off at home instead of school and I sat there in distress. I was going to have a baby and I was seventeen. I didn't know how it had happened and I didn't know what I was going to do.

My foster mother came home and was angry. She railed at me for an hour, asking me how I could be so irresponsible in not taking my pills. I sat there listening to her and when she asked me what I was thinking I told her I had never had sex, I was determined to never have sex, and I didn't know how this happened. She was infuriated by my answer and told me again how stupid it was not to take the pills. I cried and told her I had not had sex. She was exasperated and called the doctor.

After talking to the doctor she started quizzing me about the Christmas party. I told her all I remembered. She called the school and asked them to send Helen home. She made me some hot chocolate and then made a few calls. My foster father came home and was told the news. When Helen came home he quizzed her about the night of the party and then told her she could go back to school. They told her to keep this whole business quiet. She left and my foster parents told me they had arranged for me to go to a clinic where they would take care of everything. They told me there was nothing to worry about. My foster mother said they would take me to the doctor's office for some paperwork and then we would go to the Friendly Clinic. I would be home that night with this whole nightmare behind me. I wondered how that would be possible when I was going to have a baby. I was going to be a mother. She told me to clean up and fix my makeup and we would leave after lunch.

We ate lunch in silence and I tried to absorb the fact that I had a baby inside of me. I had no appetite but I relaxed a bit because my foster parents were taking care of things and were no longer angry. We left for the doctor's office and my foster dad stayed in the car. I sat in the waiting room while my foster mother talked to the doctor. The doctor called me in and asked my mother to wait outside. The doctor told me she had made arrangements for me to go to the Friendly Clinic to have an abortion and afterward I would no longer be pregnant. I asked her what would happen to the baby. She said at this stage it wasn't really a baby, just a blob of tissue. I was having difficulty absorbing all of this. That morning I was having a baby and now I just had a blob of tissue. She asked me if I understood and I nodded. She told me to wait outside and send my mother in. I sat down outside beside a woman who was reading a magazine. She looked up as I sat down. She asked me if I was all right. I told her that morning I was going to have a baby and now I had a blob of tissue. I didn't know what I had done to cause this. She asked me a few more questions and realized what was going on. She said if I wanted to save this baby which was inside of me, I should not step inside the doors of the Friendly Clinic. They would kill the baby. I was numb when the realization of what I was doing hit me. Visions of my mother praying for her children flooded my heart and when my foster mother reappeared, I told her I didn't want to go to the clinic. She told me this needed to be done right away before anyone found out. I told her I needed to protect my baby and needed time to think things through. She was angry and stalked out. My foster father came in and demanded that I come with them. I was scared because I had never crossed them before, but I didn't want to kill my baby. He left when he realized he was not going to persuade me.

The woman beside me asked if I needed a ride and said she would take me anywhere I wanted to go. She was called in to see the doctor and I waited for her. She asked me if I would like something to eat and since I had not eaten at lunchtime I agreed to go to a little café with her. She ordered a sandwich and some tea and allowed me to gather my thoughts before talking again. I told her my whole sad story including the strangeness at the Christmas party. She helped me see that I had probably been drugged and raped. She also told me I had the right to decide to keep my baby and there were places and people who would help me all the way. She asked me if I went to church and I told her we only went at Christmas and a few other times. She invited me to go to with her and I told her I would like that. We talked for about an hour and then she drove me home.

I was met with angry looks when I went through the front door.

Immediately there were questions as to where I had been, who I had been with, and what I was going to do. My foster mother asked me if I had come to my senses yet and if she should make a new appointment for the next day. I told her I didn't need an appointment. I was not sure what I wanted to do but I didn't like the idea of killing my baby. My foster mother told me there was no baby yet and because we had caught it early, it was still just a pregnancy. She said the pregnancy could be terminated before it became a baby. I considered her words. They sounded reasonable but did not make sense to me. I promised to think about it and went to my room. I was confused and decided to call Mrs. Alford, my new friend from the doctor's office. She agreed to meet me the next day at the café, which wasn't far from my home. Helen came home and dropped by to see if I was all right. She had told the kids at school I had the flu and I could stay home for a few days if I wanted. She asked me when I was going to have it taken care of. I just shook my head. I really didn't know what I was going to do.

Next morning, as usual I was feeling pretty sick when I first woke up, but by eleven the nausea had passed and I called Mrs. Alford. We met at the café again and she told me the name of a Christian pregnancy center where I could get help and information. She said she would take me there if I wanted. After lunch we drove to a pretty building in the center of town. I was nervous going in but as soon as I was through the door, a woman with a wide smile greeted me and asked if she could help me. I told her I was pregnant and needed some information. She introduced me to another woman who invited me to sit down with her and tell her what I wanted to know. I asked if Mrs. Alford could stay with me and we were ushered into a room which had pretty flowers and comfy chairs. We sat down and Mrs. Roberts, the woman we had been introduced to, told us that the pregnancy center would help in any way they could. She asked me if Mrs Alford was my mother and I told her that she was a friend.

Mrs. Roberts and proceeded to tell us about the clinic. She said they believed in the sanctity of life and would never under any circumstances recommend an abortion. I was relieved to hear that but asked what I should do if my foster parents insisted. She told me I had the right to make my own decision about the baby. She asked me if I knew where my birth parents were; I told her my mother was dead and I did not know where my father was. She told me the clinic was a private one, run by Christians who believe

God is the creator of life. He created the earth, the sun, the moon, and all the planets and stars. He created the first man and woman, two genders who would join together to procreate, a just and merciful God. Because his created beings sinned against him, he in his infinite mercy sent his only begotten Son to earth to be born of a virgin, to live, to preach his word to everyone he met, and to die at the hands of wicked men. This was because God's perfect justice demanded a substitute for mankind who was himself perfect. Jesus was that perfect man and he gladly went to the cross to bear the sins of all who would believe in him and be saved. God did this because of his great love for his people.

I was amazed. She spoke as if she actually knew this God. I had only heard his name spoken as a curse word or by the priest in the church at Christmas. She asked me what my plans were for my baby and myself. I told her my foster parents had made an appointment for me at the Friendly Clinic the previous day and I had refused to go because I wasn't sure how they would take care of the baby. She told me the only thing they do there is abortions and they do not take care of babies. I was sure then I did not want to go there, but I still did not know what to do. I asked Mrs. Roberts if they took care of babies. She told me they take care of mothers and teach mothers how to take care of babies. That sounded more positive. I asked what I needed to do next.

Mrs. Roberts lifted a book and showed me the different stages of growth a baby would go through. It was amazing. She showed me what size a baby would be at six weeks and at eight weeks. She asked me if I would like to have a sonogram to verify the age of the baby. I wasn't sure if my foster parents would agree to pay for one but she said they were free. She asked if I wanted to ask if they wanted to come with me to see the baby. I couldn't wait to tell them and we made arrangements to come back later. Mrs. Alford drove me home and told me to call her if I needed a ride the following day. I was excited and as soon as my foster parents came home I told them about this other clinic where they would help me with the baby. Instead of being glad, they were furious and angry, telling me if I continued with this madness my life would be over, that all the money they had invested in me would be wasted. I soon realized they were not going to help me with the baby and my growing uneasiness was brought to fruition when they agreed that if I would not go through with the abortion, I was on my own. They told me I had until the following Monday to decide what my future would be: have an abortion, stay with them, and go to college, or keep this baby, move out on my own, and make my own way in the world. It was like a death sentence. How could I possibly make it on my own? Maybe I should have an abortion. I spent the rest of the day in my room, coming out only once to eat dinner and meet with the hard, stony looks. Helen was the only one to speak and she told me I had ruined everything. We were supposed to go to college together and I was being selfish. She couldn't believe I was being so obstinate and foolhardy. What did I think would happen at school when everyone found out? She would be the laughing stock of the school. I wondered how that would be when it was me who was pregnant but I considered it wise to keep my mouth shut.

Chapter 4

I CALLED MRS. ALFORD TO SEE IF SHE WAS BUSY THE next day and she agreed to pick me up at noon to talk. I spent a lonely evening and a restless night in my room. In the morning I decided to retrieve my Bible from its hiding place. It had two sections so I decided to read the second section, and I read all about Jesus' birth just like Mrs. Roberts had told me. I read and read. It was amazing and Mrs. Roberts said it was true. I wondered if I was one of the people Jesus had died for. I wondered if my baby was and, if so, what was my responsibility. I thought if the baby was God's then would it matter if he or she was killed. Did God give me this child so I would protect and take care of him or her? I prayed to God and asked him to help me. I was so conflicted that I could not make a decision. I was angry at one point because of the guy at the party, and renewed my decision to never trust a man. I didn't venture out of my room until it was time to leave. No one was around as I left so there was no confrontation.

We went back to the café, which was busier than usual. The waitress told us her co-worker was going to be moving in a few weeks and was away to see her new place that day so she was on her own. I had some money so I offered to buy lunch that day. Mrs. Alford refused and said I was doing her a favor, that she had lost her husband a few months ago and was very lonely. She asked me if I would like to come to her home for dinner that night. I thought of the situation at home and agreed. I told her I had been thinking that maybe I should have an abortion, and she told me there are many things that can happen with an abortion and I shouldn't make up my mind yet. She let me talk and was never judgmental about what I said. She told me about the emotional distress that happens after an abortion and about how sometimes the treatments used for abortion do not work. She asked me if she could pray with me, and she did just like my mother used to. On the way home she invited me to go to church with her the next day. I thought I'd like to do that because I was not looking forward to spending the day with my family.

At home, we sat in silence until bedtime and then I went to my room, wondering if they would really make me move out. I read from my Bible again and learned about Jesus calling people to follow him. I wondered why my mother had never read it to me—or had she? Those scary days were so far away and yet these days did not seem any better. What was I going to do if I had to move out? Should I have the abortion and keep everyone happy just so I could stay here and go to college with Helen. Was our friendship over regardless? Was the friendship worth saving if she expected me to do something against my will? I finally fell asleep and when I went into the kitchen for breakfast, I found that everyone was gone.

I called Mrs. Alford to see if she could come for me and she was waiting for my call. Everyone at her church spoke to me as if they had been waiting for me. I felt more at home there than in my own home. We sang some songs from a book, then a man (I found out later he was the pastor) read from the Bible and for about forty-five minutes explained what he had read. It was great. I had wondered as I read my Bible if there was anyone who would know what it all meant. Afterward when we were on the way out the pastor shook my hand, told me I was very welcome, and if I needed anything I could just call him. He gave me a card with his telephone number on it. Mrs. Alford drove me to her home and we ate lunch. She told me if I ever needed anywhere to stay her home was there. I felt so secure and safe there. After lunch she drove me home and there was still no sign of my family. I found a note which I had missed earlier saying they would be gone for a few days to allow me time to make up my mind whether I would be staying or moving out. They did not want to discuss the matter anymore, and if I decided to go against their wishes they would expect me to be gone when they came back. I was devastated. I had wanted to talk to my parents to try to explain why I did not want to kill my baby but they obviously did not want any more discussion. I had to make a decision. I looked around at the house which had been my home for the last few years and knew I had nothing if I walked away. I sat down and was silently weeping when the doorbell rang. I went to the door and there was Mrs. Alford, who had waited to see if I was all right. She put her arms around me and, sobbing, I showed her the note. She held me for quite a while and then asked if she could pray with me. I nodded and she asked God to help me make my decision. She said she would leave me and I could call her when I had made my decision, or I could just come with her and spend the day with her. I told her I needed time to think and she left.

I thought about the baby inside of me. The pastor had said that Jesus had taken the little children on his lap and said the kingdom of heaven was made up of them. Jesus was God's son and he loved little children. How could I kill one so I could stay here? How could I give birth to one when I had nothing to give? I couldn't take care of a baby, not yet anyway. I could get rid of it and go to college. It! It wasn't an it. He or she was a living person. I knew in that moment I couldn't kill. I packed a few clothes and my Bible and a few other things. I wasn't sure what I could take with me. I called Mrs. Alford and asked her if I could stay with her for a few days until I figured out what to do. She was waiting for my call and came at once. She told me I could stay as long as I wanted. She would give me a ride to school each morning and pick me up. She was like an angel standing by my side.

We talked all afternoon and she asked me if I wanted to go back to church with her that evening. I did and the pastor read a part of the Bible which I had read. It was called Romans and was about an apostle called Paul. I was happy as I followed along while he explained each verse. That is what I had longed for. Paul had been through many trials and I felt a kindred spirit with him. The pastor explained that even though Paul had been through many of the hardships encountered in the human experience, such as trouble, persecution, famine, nakedness, violence, prison, and almost death, he had God on his side. Even after all these things, Paul wrote, "We are more than conquerors through Him who loved us." The pastor told us when we belong to Jesus we can overcome many of the stresses of life because Jesus is there beside us. In that moment I knew I needed Jesus in my life. I was overcome with the realization that my mother had coped with the unbelievable situation she had to live in because she knew Jesus. I had heard her pray in his name. I was so deep in my thought I didn't realize the service was over and most people had left. Mrs. Alford was sitting on the seat beside me, quietly waiting. When I looked up, she asked me if I was all right and I told her I needed Jesus. I saw tears in her eyes as she answered, "I know you do. Just ask him." As I sat there beside her I asked Jesus to be in my life just as he had been in Paul's and help me make sense of my situation.

As we left, I felt an overwhelming wave of contentment like I had never felt in my life. Mrs. Alford invited me to live with her as a companion and help her with the housework in lieu of rent. She said she had been lonely since her husband passed and would love the company. I knew then that God had sent her that day in the doctor's office to guide me through this difficult time. I thought about my family and felt no anger. I knew I needed to talk to them and thank them for all they had done for me. I went to bed that night a changed person. I was going to be the best mother I could possibly be. Life was good and when I was alone in my room I would think about that other life and wonder why it was allowed to happen. My friends in church were always thankful for everything, good or bad, and I secretly wondered if they would have been thankful had they lived my life. I could never find the courage to share any of that with dear Mrs. Alford or any of the other dear people in that church group. Satan started in at once with negative thoughts about God's love for His people. Was I really one of those people God had chosen to love? Did I really believe that God would have allowed me to be born into my birth family if I was a chosen vessel for God, I would have had a better deal in life. I consoled myself with the thought that if I kept company with those who were his then some of his blessings would filter through to me. I slept better than I had for some time and woke up refreshed the next morning.

Mrs. Alford had breakfast ready when I emerged from the bathroom and we sat down together. She asked me if I wanted to thank God for the food or if I wanted her to do it. I asked if she would and when she had finished she asked me if there was something wrong. It was so easy to talk to her so I told her of my misgivings and she said that the negative thoughts were probably just the old devil trying to take away my joy. We had quite a long conversationwhich ended when I told her I would like to thank God for choosing me. It was so easy to talk to God when I knew that everything which happened to me was for my good. I didn't know how but I believed it. I knew that God would do the rest. I was happier than I had been in my entire life. What I didn't know was that my trials were just beginning. Some of the girls in our group asked me where Helen was. I didn't know what to say. They looked at me with questioning expressions when I shrugged. I left it at that and walked to my class. It was a long, strange day without Helen. None of the teachers asked about her so they must have been informed that she would not be there. I tried to avoid the girls as much as possible simply because I did not know what to tell them.

At last the day ended and when Mrs. Alford arrived I asked her if she would drop me off at the café for a few minutes. I applied for the job at the café and the owner was happy for me to start the following week. I would work every evening and Saturday from 9:00 a.m. to 1:00 p.m. I would get paid every Saturday when I finished work. I would be off Sundays so I could go to church. On the way out the door I said "Thank you Lord" because I knew without a doubt that God was making this all possible. The rest of the week was uneventful. One of the teachers told us Helen was away visiting the university which she wanted to attend and encouraged us to do the same. I received some questioning looks from my friends and one asked me why I hadn't gone with Helen. I told her I was not going to college yet and she seemed satisfied with that answer. I realized I was going to need God's help in the next few months because I was not sure what Helen was going to say. I resolved to concentrate on my grades and do the best I could. During my free period I did homework in the library and after school, I rode home with Mrs. Alford, changed into my uniform, and headed to the café. Mrs. Alford always asked if she could drop me off but I needed the exercise so I refused her help and told her I might need help later when my baby grew bigger. I silently talked to God often that week and in the weeks to come.

The next week was a little awkward. Helen tried to walk past me but I stopped her and asked her how things had gone the previous week. She didn't answer at first and then, after a long look at me, she told me everything was set for the fall. She asked me what I was going to do and I told her I would eventually go to college but I didn't know when. She seemed genuinely happy I was speaking to her and we walked together to class. That in itself seemed to quieten all the questions from our friends and life went smoothly.

I learned quickly at the café and when I asked if I could have time off to go to doctor's appointments, the owner said it was not a problem if I let him know the week before. He also told me that as the clinic was within walking distance, I could probably go on my lunch time and not lose any time. I was so glad. I wanted to save as much money as I could for my education and I was going to need a lot to take care of my baby. The following day I had Mrs. Alford drive me and we stopped by the clinic. It was the same place I had been to before. I had all the papers and they encouraged me to have a sonogram as soon as I could. Those people were so loving, and not at all like people in the doctor's office. They even helped with diapers and baby clothes. I couldn't believe how much help there would be, and even Mrs. Alford was amazed. She dropped me off at the café and insisted on coming back at 8:30 to bring me home. When I got home we prayed together and thanked God for providing such a place.

A doctor and a nurse came on Thursdays to perform the sonograms. I said I would talk to someone at school to see if I could leave for leave school for that, the following Thursday. Mrs. Alford suggested I talk to the school nurse to see if she would arrange time off without telling anyone about the pregnancy. She offered to talk to the nurse for me but I knew the nurse was nice and might understand and help me. I saw her the next day and she said there would be no problem. She wrote a note and put it on her notice board so she could inform the teacher on Thursday morning.

On Thursday we drove to the clinic and they allowed Mrs. Alford to come into the sonogram room while they did the procedure. It was amazing. The nurse showed us the little blip on the screen which indicated the baby's heart. It was beating very fast. So was mine. She measured the length of the baby's legs and head. I looked at Mrs. Alford with blurry eyes and saw she was weeping too. I wished so much that my foster parents could have been here, but nothing could mar my joy at that moment. I thought of my dear mother and vowed to myself and God I would be the best mother I could be. When I saw the doctor, he was able to tell me approximately when my baby would be born: September 21. I still had a notion in my head that I could go to college but hearing the date of my baby's birth made me realize college was out of the question. I was going to be a mother and have a child to care for. Suddenly I was overwhelmed with the responsibility of it all and I started sobbing. The doctor put his arm around me and sent the nurse to get Mrs. Alford. She was worried there was something wrong and hugged me when I told her I didn't think I could do this. She squeezed me tightly and said, "We'll do it together, sweetie." I loved her so much at that moment. God had indeed sent an angel to see me through my trials.

I continued to go to the clinic every week and each month I would see the doctor. The staff showed us videos about pregnancy, mothering, feeding, and caring for a baby. We also had devotions each week and homework to do. We had a worksheet to fill out as we watched the video and the homework was usually a recap of this information. We were given the devotion sheet and a scripture verse to learn. The following week we were given points for doing our homework, learning the scripture, and being on time. If we had been to church we would get another point. If we showed our pay stub we received a point. For every point received we were given a baby buck to spend at a little store that had diapers, clothes, formula, and even car seats and cribs. It was an answer to my prayer. They assured me they would help every step of the way until my baby was eighteen months-old. I had never known such places existed but knew that it was God's provision for the little soul which lived inside of me.

I discovered that Mrs. Alford was also a talented seamstress and when my uniform got a little tight she was able to make it fit again. I bought another uniform which relieved the daily washing. My boss allowed me to go home early some nights when we were not busy and a few times he asked me to close. That encouraged me because it meant he trusted me. I had some regular customers who came every week and gave me big tips. I opened a bank account and saved all I could. My boss allowed me to eat free from the café menu and Mrs. Alford refused point blank to take any money from me. She had a lunch ready for me every day for school so I wouldn't have to pay for that. It made me happy to see my bank account growing as well as my baby buck account. I could see that I was actually going to be able to do this with God's help. I was a bit worried that my church friends would not want to know me when it became obvious I was pregnant, but I need not have worried. They were so helpful and every so often someone would bring a baby item for me to store away.

Chapter 5

HELEN REMAINED FRIENDS WITH ME TOO AFTER A couple of weeks of discomfort. She asked me quite often if I was doing all right or if I needed anything. She never mentioned her parents and neither did I. One day toward the end of the school year, she brought me a box containing some things I had left. I told her I didn't know what I should take when I left. She hugged me and said she was sorry for the way things had turned out. She had asked her parents if I could come back but they were adamant that I should never cross their door again. She was so embarrassed to tell me and I loved her for that. There were a lot of parties towards the end of the year and I noticed she was not showing any interest in them. We talked about it once and she told me she felt responsible for what had happened to me. I insisted she should not carry that burden, that I was fine, and that God had used the experience to draw me to him. She told me she knew that there was something different about me since I left her home. I shared with her the way in which God had made me realize that he was in control and that knowing his son was more important than any other thing in the world. I told her what I had heard in church and what I had read in the Bible. She was so interested that I dared to ask her if she wanted to come to church with us. She said she might. She had been different too since I left her home, more caring and thoughtful of others. She was talking to girls who she would have ignored or ridiculed before. It was amazing and it made life much more bearable than if she had been her old self. She asked me what church I went to before leaving that day.

Praise the Lord, there were no unexpected problems with my pregnancy and every month the doctor would smile and say everything was well and the baby was growing. I could tell that myself because Mrs. Alford's skillful sewing could not make my clothes stretch any farther. The last week of school I was determined to go shopping for new clothes the following week with Mrs. Alford. We were going to go on the Monday and get it all done before I started work. We went to church as usual and the pastor announced that there would be a potluck dinner after church in the fellowship hall. I looked at Mrs. Alford because I knew she had not cooked anything. She had this funny look and I thought she had just forgotten. After the service we were walking out and I saw Helen. She came. I had tears in my eyes as I went to talk to her. I had been praying that she would come. I invited her to the dinner and she agreed to stay. We went into the fellowship hall and in the front were mountains of boxes and packages. I had no idea what they were for. I helped to serve the dinner as I usually did but Mrs. Alford and some of the other women told me to go sit with my friend. Helen was quiet as we ate and then the pastor stood up and asked me to come to the front. I did not have an inkling about what was going to happen. He shook my hand and said, "These are for you, from your friends. We hope this will help as the time for your baby's birth draws nigh. We know you are concerned about the cost and wanted to help in a small way." I was crying before he finished talking. I could not believe that all this stuff had been brought by these people for me. The pastor called Mrs. Alford up and she helped me to my seat. Everyone started clapping their hands. It took me a while to subdue the emotion and thank everyone. They told me I did not need to open the gifts there but I could take them home to open so I could organize and put them away in some kind of order. I had difficulty talking and thanking them. They made it easier as they started coming and hugging me and telling me they loved me and my baby. I noticed Helen had tears running down her cheeks, and that was an unusual sight because she was always much in control of her emotions. She helped carry the gifts to the car and even brought some herself to Mrs. Alford's in her car.

What a day! Helen stayed all afternoon and our conversation was mostly about the Lord and how he had given his life in order to save us. His provision is more abundant than we could ever ask or think. Helen had many questions and said she would like to come back the following Sunday.

She had realized I worked at the café and started coming there every so often for lunch. She would give me a twenty dollar bill as a tip, saying I needed it more than she did. Again I thanked God for his provision. She came all summer every Friday and when we had time we would talk. She came to church every Sunday and sat by us, and she spent every Sunday afternoon at Mrs. Alford's discussing the scriptures.

One Sunday toward the end of the summer she asked if we would pray for her because she needed to be saved. I was overwhelmed with joy that my best friend believed in my Jesus. I couldn't find the words. Mrs. Alford prayed and we held hands and Helen prayed and by then I had found my tongue. We all cried and laughed together. It was wonderful. She did not want to go home. She asked us to pray for her as she told her parents because she did not know what their reaction would be. We said we would and off she went. I hugged Mrs. Alford and thanked her again for helping me that day in the doctor's office. She said it was all in God's plan. She was emotional as she in turn thanked me for trusting her and told me I had changed her life. She said I was the daughter she never had and I could call her Mom so long as I agreed it would not take away from my memories of my own mother. I thought it would be all right. She hugged me so tightly I could barely breathe. She then told me she would help me go to college and even babysit our baby while I attended classes. I loved it when she said our baby. She was indeed just like a mom to me. September came and Helen moved quite far away to attend university. Our pastor knew someone in the area and gave Helen the address of a church in case she wanted to attend services there. She said she would look it up as soon as she got there. I missed her after one day. Then something else happened which took up my full attention: a contraction. Whoa! It was too soon for this.

During the summer I had been working mornings in the café and finishing at four, and it was only two o'clock and the café was full. Another waitress came in for a couple of hours at lunchtime and she was about to leave. Thankfully, the contraction was short but it sure took by breath away. I was able to continue working till the end of my shift but I told Mom when I reached home. She told me to talk to my doctor in the morning. I had two more contractions that evening but slept well. Next day I saw the doctor and he told me to take it easy. I went back to the café and my boss had already found someone to fill in for me for a couple of months. We had talked about it some time before and I was thrilled that he had acted on it. I was to work till the end of the week, if I could and the new person would start the following Monday. If at any time I needed to go home my boss would have the new waitress come in to cover for me.. The week went quickly and I was happy to stay home and pack and repack my hospital bag. It was quite a chore moving around at that stage but I was happy to know I would soon meet my baby.

September 21 came and went. I thought there was something wrong. I was still having contractions, sometimes for half an hour but they always stopped. Mom kept assuring me that everything was all right. We went to the clinic on the twenty-third, and the doctor told me that I was starting to dilate. He said if the contractions came and stayed and were five minutes apart, I should make my way to the hospital. The contractions were pretty scary and sometimes I thought they would never stop but Mom would hold my hand and breathe with me. On the twenty-fifth, I awoke with a very strong contraction. I got up and started walking around because that seemed to help but they were coming very fast. I drank some water and continued to walk. Mom woke up at seven and wanted to make me some breakfast but I didn't have time to eat between contractions. Mom told me we should go to the hospital, so I took a quick shower and we were on our way. At the hospital, things moved quickly and before long I was in my room. The nurse who examined me told me I was dilated to five. She said I was halfway there. I was expecting labor to go on for twenty-four hours but by eleven the nurse said the doctor was on his way. I listened to my baby on the monitor and watched the graph of the heartbeat, which was being printed on paper coming out of the monitor. My mom was able to stay with me the whole time and hold my hand. I was so grateful for that. The nurse asked me if I knew whether the baby was a boy or a girl and if I had a name. I told her that if she was a girl, I did not have a name. I wished that I had known my birth mother's name but I didn't. My baby was a boy and he was born at 12:30 p.m. I wished by brother Bobby could have been there to see my baby. I knew then what his name was going to be: Robert Swanson. As I said the name over and over to myself, I thought maybe it was too grand for a little tiny baby. Then I thought he will grow and he will be like my brother, Bobby. I wondered where he was, lonely and isolated somewhere. I wondered if he ever found Anna again. The next couple of days were a whirlwind of excitement. The women from the clinic came and brought gifts for the baby and encouraged me to come see them as soon as I could. They had more things to teach me, and wanted to be involved in raising my little one. Bobby nursed like a champ and the doctor allowed me to go home after a couple of days. Mom buzzed around and stayed busy all day long. She was so happy to have a baby in her home. I was happy too. Every time I looked at my baby, I felt such a surge of emotion that sometimes I would cry from sheer joy. My boss from the café came one day and brought several gifts from customers. It amazed me how generous and kind everyone I knew was to me and my infant.

Three weeks later I felt strong enough to go back to the clinic, and everyone crowded around to see Bobby. I watched a video which encouraged me to wear my baby and showed me how I could start doing little things around the house again. We prayed together and had devotions. Our devotions centered on the story of Jesus' disciples trying to turn people away from Jesus because they had little children. Jesus told them to bring the little children to him and said, "For of such is the kingdom of heaven. Except a man become as a little child he cannot enter the kingdom of heaven." I remembered the day God touched my heart and drew me to himself and I did feel like a little child being wrapped up in a father's arms. I looked at my baby and prayed that he would become a godly young man when he grew up and that God would give me the wisdom I needed to teach him the Bible.

Another three weeks and I went back to work in the café. We were busier coming up to the holidays and the big shopping season. There were three of us on at lunch times. Mom would bring Bobby to the café and I would feed him as I ate my lunch. He was a good little baby and Mom loved taking care of him. At home I stayed busy with the extra washing, and I persuaded Mom to teach me how to cook. That was fun, although sometimes things did not turn out quite the way there were supposed to. We laughed a lot and enjoyed each other's company. I thought about my brothers and sister a lot those days and wondered what had happened to each one. Mom told me there was no reason I couldn't go to college like I had planned. There was a junior college in the next town and she could babysit just like grandmas do. I thought about it a lot. I wondered if it was feasible as I would not be able to work. I had some savings but would it be enough? I voiced my thoughts to Mom and she said she was sure things could be worked out.

Thanksgiving came and Mom's sister Grace and her husband came to stay for a few days. Grace was interested in me and asked many questions. When she heard I wanted to go to college she suggested I apply for grants and scholarships. She said she would help me find the ones I would need, but I would not be able to use them until the following year. That night before I went to bed I said a prayer to God to thank him for sending this woman with all this information. I felt that college was almost within my grasp. A couple of weeks later, Grace called and gave me quite a few addresses where I could inquire about grants. She said someone from her church had mentioned something about a scholarship for abandoned children and she would have to find out more about it. I was taken aback at that but when I thought about it that was exactly what I was: abandoned. Mom, always quick to see a change in my expression, said, "Don't worry child. God has not abandoned you and neither will I." I loved that woman so much. The next time we went to church her friend Myra gave me a hug and said, "The Lord has laid it on my heart to pray for you in regards to furthering your education" I thought Mom had said something to her but later she told me she had not talked to her about that subject at all. Every so often, Myra would bring a little gift for me: a little calendar or a book of sayings about friendship. I read them repeatedly until I had almost memorized them. Every time I opened the book, I would think of Myra and know she cared for me. Life was good and when I was alone in my room at night, I would think about that other life and wonder why it was allowed to happen.

Grace called one day and told her sister she had great news for me. She had found out more about the scholarship and was in the process of getting the information for me. Those two sisters were wonderful; they owed me nothing but acted as if I were their sole responsibility. I felt so loved, but it reminded me of my mother and all my regrets about her flooded back into my thoughts. Sometimes Mrs. Alford and I would talk in the evenings and as I became more comfortable with her, the subjects became more varied. We talked a lot about honoring parents. I certainly had not honored my mother and would never be able to forgive my father for what he had done. I kept these thoughts bottled up inside me. Mrs. Alford was nurturing and I never felt she was probing. Grace brought the paperwork and helped me fill it out. It was a scholarship for children who had been abandoned by their parents and it paid all the tuition for four years of college. I knew I could afford to pay for the supplies so I became excited. I would have to keep up a 3.5 grade point average and I was certain I could do that. Mom and her sister Grace could not have been more helpful if I had been their own child. We mailed the application with great ceremony and when we came back home they both prayed that everything would work out.

A few weeks later a thin large-business size envelope arrived for me. I did not get mail often so I looked at it for quite a while before opening it. I left it on the little table beside the couch. Mrs. Alford came home from her walk and saw it. She looked at me and looked at the letter and had a questioning look on her face but said nothing. I told her I was afraid to open it because I did not want to know the bad news yet. She hugged me and I saw a glisten in her eye as she lifted the letter, handed it to me, and told me she believed everything was going to work for me; if things did not work out this time then something else would come along. I opened the letter and I think I must have read the words a dozen times before it dawned on me that I met the standards for the scholarship and had an interview in January. I was told about two different universities, each of which had a place for this particular scholarship. All I needed were letters of recommendation from two teachers. I was thrilled I had qualified but devastated because the closest university was in Newtownville, which was one hundred miles away. There was no way I could go. I chided myself for even thinking it was possible. Mom had a puzzled look on her face and I knew she was waiting for me to tell her the news. I told her I had been given the scholarship but it was for university not junior college. She was as disappointed as I was and tried to think of ways I could go. She even suggested I leave Bobby with her and go. I considered that for about a second and, as much as I loved Mom, there was no way I would live so far away from my precious son.

Grace had invited us to her home for Christmas. We were to spend my five days off with her and her family. I found out that packing for a small child takes more time and space than for an adult. Their church was having a service on Christmas morning and we were invited to that as well. The service was remarkable because there were so many children there all waiting till after church to get their gifts. I thought about the last few Christmases and marveled at their happy faces. I could not believe they could be happy waiting until after church to get their gifts but here they were all smiling and happy, singing and reciting all their various pieces. It was truly memorable, not at all like the Christmas service I had attended with my foster family. It was warm and happy and I felt so much joy that it drove away the disappointing thoughts about the scholarship.

Grace's home was beautiful and there was a certain comfortable feeling about it not like the store window which had been my foster home. Dinner was exceptional. Grace's children had all arrived for church service and there was such a crowd of bustling people I felt a little out of place. Grace had five children and with their spouses and children there were twenty-seven of us sitting at the meal, laughing and talking and having a wonderful time. Bobby must have felt the warmth too because he slept all the way through dinner. After dinner Grace's two daughters told us to relax and they would clear up the dishes. When they were finished we had a gift exchange. Mom had gifts for everyone and told them they were from both of us. She winked at me as she handed them to me to pass around. It was not at all like the grand affair I had experienced with my foster family, where no expense was spared, but this was truly the best day I had ever experienced. Grace's husband John was a wonderful person and so were her sons and sons-in-law. They joked with one another, and teased and laughed with such good humor. It was so different from the exchanges I remembered from my younger days between my father and brothers. This family gave me hope there were actually some men who loved their wives. They were kind and loving to their children and even offered to help by holding Bobby when I was opening my gifts. I could not help but compare Grace's husband John, to my birth father and when I thought about him, a shudder passed through my body. John saw me and thought I was cold. He jumped up and brought me a soft blanket to wrap around my shoulders. I was not really cold but his gesture was so full of loving care I accepted it with gladness. The whole family made me feel as if I belonged, and I have to say that belonging is truly one of the most blessed of situations. Later on at home in my room I thanked God for the day and for all it had meant to me.

The next morning was interesting, because two of Grace's children were staying over with the five grand-children. What a time we had sorting the bathroom rotation and getting breakfast. While the younger children played with their toys Sharen, Grace's oldest daughter, told us her husband

Steve, who had been in the reserves, had been mobilized and was leaving soon for his tour of duty. She hoped her Aunt Lori (Mrs. Alford) would move in with her for company but had not realized Bobby and I lived with her now. She was taking some classes at the university and needed someone she could trust to have at home with the children. She asked if I had any plans and I told her I didn't think so. Grace jumped in and told her I wanted to go to university and that Mom was going to help me with Bobby. Sharen understood and let the subject drop. I didn't know what to think. I didn't want to keep Mom from helping her niece but I had nowhere else to go. Then Grace asked me if I had heard anything from the scholarship people. I told her that I had been given a four-year scholarship but it was for university and not junior college. The closest university was 100 miles away in Newtownville. I was still going to try to figure out a way to attend the college and thanked her for all she had done. Grace kept looking at her daughter as we spoke.

Sharen was jumping up and down in her seat and finally said, "I live in Newtownville and that university is where I'm taking my classes. You must all come and live with me. My mom told me things would work out. Please, oh please come and live with me. Steve is going to be gone for at least two years and I would love your company. Aunt Lori, please."

Grace jumped in and said "Of course you must go. It's the perfect solution for everyone. God had this all worked out before we even knew what was happening." She was right of course.

Mom just looked at me with a questioning look and I didn't know what to say. I was nauseous with excitement at the thought of being able to go, but wasn't sure if it was what Mom wanted. She let me know at once that she would only go if I wanted to. I hugged her and then Sharen hugged her and before she sat down Grace hugged her. She explained the situation a little more. Steve had to go for training and could live at home for a few more months but then he would be overseas. He figured he would be leaving toward the end of May, so that gave us plenty of time to figure out what we needed to bring. She told us she had two rooms which she was not using. They both had bedroom furniture but she had given away her crib. We spent the rest of that day writing lists and comparing notes. I was excited and I could see Mom was too. Mom told me that as soon as we reached home I should get the application in the mail. I realized I needed the teachers' letters so I decided that the morning after we arrived home, I would visit my school.

That morning, before I left we prayed together and thanked God for his provision and asked him to guide me as I requested the necessary letters. Mom watched Bobby while I walked to the school. I went over and over in my mind what I needed to say and which teachers I was going to request the letters from. The only one I was worried about was the principal. I arrived at the school and was told by the secretary to wait in the hall. I felt like a student who had done something wrong.

I was pleasantly surprised when the principal came out and asked me to come in. He asked me how I was doing and if I was well. Then he asked if there was something he could do for me. I took a deep breath and told him I had been awarded a four-year scholarship for the university in Newtownville but I needed a letter from him and from two of my former teachers to send with the application. He told me it was no problem and he would be glad to write a letter for me. He asked me which teachers I was thinking about and I told him. He thought both teachers were there that day and together we went to their classrooms where he informed them of my request. They were both willing to write the letters and asked me how I was doing. We went back to his office where he wrote his letter and had the secretary type it on school stationery for me. He reminded me I had a prize which had never been picked up. My foster parents had told them my address had changed but I had left without giving them my new address. I told him they had asked me to leave because I was having a baby. He said a very long, "Ahhhhh" and left it there.

The prize turned out to be a book certificate for $500. I was pleased because I could give some of the money I'd saved to Mrs. Alford and use my prize to buy some of the books I needed. One of the teachers came almost at once and handed me the letter, then wished me all the best in my endeavor. The other one took a little longer but when she arrived she had a gift for me. Apparently quite a few of the teachers had collected and bought me this gift and then had no address to send it to. I walked home and on the way stopped by the café. My boss was surprised to see me as I was not scheduled that day. I told him I would have to leave later that year as I was going to university and moving to Newtownville. He was not unhappy at all but was excited I was going. As I walked I considered the things which had occurred with the last six months since I left school and marveled at God's providence. The next step was to get applications for the university and I did that before the end of the week. Then I waited. I expected it would take a while for them to answer but it took only one week and there it was in the mail. My interview was scheduled for the first week of February. I was so excited. I thought my mother would be pleased. I told my baby everything as I cuddled with him. He would look at me and open his eyes so wide. There was so much emotion passing between us. I told him how God had preserved us and provided for us, gave us a new loving family, and that I loved him so much. I thought about how God gave his son to become a man only to live a short life and die so we could be forgiven. I prayed God would preserve my son and help him grow up to do his will.

Chapter 6

THE DAY OF MY INTERVIEW WAS COLD AND I WAS nervous. Mom told me to consider how God had worked things out for me up till then and to put my faith in him. She told me that the prayer group at church was remembering me that day. Grace said she would drive me there and Mom said she would come too so I could be near Bobby. She prayed with me before we set out that morning. The interview was quite simple. They had verified everything in my paperwork and asked for the letters. There were pleased with all of them, and quickly brought the interview to an end with the welcome words, "We will grant you a place. Now it is up to you to make the best of it." I thought all the muscles in my body were going to spasm because I was so glad to hear those words. I was going to university. My mother would be happy. I wondered if she could see. I ran out to the foyer where my dear friends were waiting. Bobby was sleeping. Mrs. Alford and Grace were sitting with their heads bowed, praying quietly, not caring if anyone saw them. It amazed me because I was always so worried I would be embarrassed doing that in public. I think I had spent so much time as I was growing up worrying that somehow people would know what went on in our home, and I worked to put on an appearance of normalcy. I sat down beside them and Grace was the first to open her eyes. She saw my happy expression and said, "You got in. Oh how wonderful. I am so happy for you." They both hugged me and we went for lunch, which Grace insisted was her treat. We talked about what I would need and they told me to make a list of everything I could think of including pens, pencils, paper, and books. They were as excited as I was and it was fun trying to think about what to write on the list. The books of course depended on which classes I signed up for and that would have to wait.

Next time Grace came to visit she brought a large box which she had decorated, and on the front were the words Lillian's supplies. From that day on every time Grace came to visit, she had a pen or a box of pencils or a notebook, something to put in my box. I started adding things myself and then on my birthday I had the biggest surprise. Mom had arranged a birthday party for me. It happened during Easter break and the few friends I had from church were home from college and arrived to surprise me. They had heard I had been awarded the scholarship and were so excited. They brought me gifts to put in my box. One of the gifts was a year of daily readings from the Bible with comments from various preachers. I did not put that in my box but started that night reading them to Mom. The suggestion was to read seven or eight verses per day, but I found myself reading chapters at a time. When I came upon something which did not make sense I would ask Mom, and she would patiently explain it as far as she could. She would tell me to ask the pastor if I had more questions. I listened carefully to what the pastor said during his sermons. Sometimes, I got the idea that it did not really matter whether a person had been good or bad, a saint or a devil, because God loved that person anyway. That did not make much sense to me and my thoughts turned to my father. I thought if God loves my father then he will go to heaven and I did not want to be there. I made myself think about something else when I reached that point.

Summer was a busy time. We packed up and moved in with Sharen in the middle of June. She was so excited to see us. She was already missing her hubby, as she called him. Our rooms were quite large and mine had a door to the back garden. It was so pretty. There was a patio where I could let Bobby play. Within the week we were settled in and Bobby enjoyed playing with Sharen's kids. I had most of my stuff ready, had signed up for my classes, had bought most of my books, and had an abundance of supplies, thanks to my friends. One day when I was sitting outside watching Bobby as he scooted after his little car, I realized how wonderful my life was, how happy Bobby was, and how different it might have been. I shuddered as I thought of those moments when I had considered an abortion. I would have killed him. My thoughts quickly became tears and Mom found me sobbing uncontrollably. She asked me if I was ill. She asked me if she had offended me. She asked me if I was having second thoughts. I struggled to get control of my emotions. She put her arms around me and told me she loved me and would do anything for me. I told her she was the reason for my tears because she had made me feel that I was loved and I was overcome with the thought of what could have been. I told her I would never be able to repay her for all she and her family and her friends had done for me. She grabbed me and held me tightly and told me that I was God's answer to her prayers. She said she felt blessed to have me in her life and thought of me as her daughter. She said she didn't feel as if she had done anything to repay all the happiness I had brought to her. She told me the first few weeks might be hard as I get used to my new routine and classes, but that after that I would have a blast. That sounded so funny coming from her that I giggled. She laughed too and I was able to compose myself.

We talked often during the next few weeks and I eventually told her my whole sordid story, how I had refused to kiss my mother goodbye because she had not made the pies which she had promised and that she was dead. I believed if I had gone back to kiss her I could have prevented her death. I cried and Mom cried and then she tried to assure me that my mother's death was not my fault. She said she had not realized that things were that bad and if there was anything she could do to help, I was to ask. Then she said something which stirred up in me a resentment which was long buried: "I think we should pray for your father."

"I don't think so. He is a wicked man," I retorted.

She quietly reminded me that God died for wicked men. I considered that for a long time. Mom broke into my thoughts and asked me what I would do, as a follower of Jesus, if I met someone who asked me for help. I told her I would help him if I could. My boss at the café had told me there were two homeless men who would come to the back door of the café and I was to give them food when they dropped by. I always kept a special piece of pie for them and it made me feel good helping them. I did not have a problem helping people who needed help. My father was a different story. Mom in a very soft voice said she believed my father needed help and if I ever met up with him God would expect me to forgive him and try to help him. I had to think on that one. I had not forgiven him; I had just tried to forget him. I was silent for a long time until Bobby let me know he needed attention. I scooped him up and went to my room, still lost in the conflict going on in my head. I absentmindedly put Bobby's pants on backward and when Sharen arrived home she laughed and asked me what I was thinking when I dressed him that way. I looked at Mom, who I had been avoiding, and she said nothing. There was an awkward silence and Sharen asked if something was going on. I tried to say something and couldn't. I was so conflicted. I was angry with my father. I was angry with myself for not forgiving him because I knew it was something which would please Mom. Why was this so hard?

Sharen asked if it would be all right to pray together or if I'd rather be alone. Mom came over and hugged me and told her to go ahead. She told Sharen I had a difficult decision to make and to ask God for guidance. Sharen took one of my hands and Mom took the other. Sharen asked God to help me with my decision, and thanked him for being there for us in time of need. She thanked him for bringing Mom and me to her in her time of need and asked that he put his loving arms around me and give me wisdom in my decision. Mom said "Amen." I knew what I had to do but I did not want to do it. My father was so cruel to my mother that I didn't feel he deserved forgiveness, but what would God do? When I was able to verbalize my thoughts I asked them if God forgave murderers. Mom told me that God forgives all who come to him in faith and ask for forgiveness and that maybe my father was one of those. If God had forgiven him then why would I not. Sharen was quite puzzled and I told her that as far as I knew, my mother died from injuries inflicted by my father and he had driven off and left them all. She came over and held me tight, whispering she was sorry and that I would be safe with her. At that moment, as I thought about my treatment of my dying mother, my jealousy of Anna, my haughty attitude to my brother, the continual insults I had thrown at some of the girls in school while I was in Helen's clique, I knew God had forgiven me for all of these things. He had known about the loneliness in my heart and had in his own way given me a family. Suddenly the burden was lifted from my heart, and I knew if God could rescue me from the situation I had been in, he could help me find forgiveness in my heart. The realization that God had been in control all along was such a comfort to me. I knew even if I never met my father, I could forgive him. I felt such joy that I felt sorry for him because it was obvious he had no joy in his life. A new item was added to my bucket list that day. I was going to look for my father and find out if he had ever heard the good news of the gospel.

What a relief that was to me. I felt I had been carrying that yoke for a long time, always afraid that what had happened in my family would become known and I would be despised. Instead, I had voluntarily told both of these dear people and they loved me more because of it. I had a new purpose in my life as I realized that maybe I was the one person God had appointed to tell my father the good news of the gospel.

Many times during the remainder of that summer I rehearsed the words I would say to my father. I prayed every day that God would give me the opportunity. We started going to church with Sharen and although there were few people, most of them older, the church had a warm and loving atmosphere. I missed the girls from Mom's church but found that these dear people had such a love for God and his word, they made it easy to love them. They would often on a Sunday invite all of us for lunch and we would spend the afternoon with them. When Sharen would try to reciprocate, they would refuse and tell her she was too busy and they had nothing else to do. Bobby had so much fun going from one to the other showing them his treasures, and they loved that he was such an outgoing and engaging child. Every night I thanked God for his love to me and Bobby, and for bringing me into his fold.

Chapter 7

THE FIRST DAY OF CLASSES ARRIVED AND I TRIED TO make sure Mom had everything she needed for Bobby. She finally told me to stop fussing and go or I would be late. I set off with a little trepidation, wondering what my day would be like. My first class was Government and I thought it would be a relatively easy class. I had done well in school and was confident I would have no problems. The professor started the class by introducing himself and asking us to introduce ourselves and tell the class a little about ourselves. That took me by surprise and I didn't have much time to think about what to say. The first person told us his name and then said he was the son of the president of one of the large manufacturing plants in that county, he had been captain of his high school football team for two years, his brother was a chemist in a well-known pharmaceutical company, and his goal was to take over from his father when he retired. Next was a girl who said she had been the team leader of the swim club in her school and they were first in the championship meets at the last gala. She said her Mom was a nurse and she was thinking she would like to be a doctor.

Then it was me. My head was swimming, I said "My name is Lillian and I have a little boy." I couldn't think of another thing to say so I sat down quickly. The professor, smirking, said "OK then, moving on." I barely heard what was said after that. I wanted to bury my head somewhere or stand up again and explain everything, about how I became pregnant, and that I wasn't what they might think me to be. The opportunity was gone. I should have said something else and I didn't. I asked God to help me because I had suddenly lost my confidence. The professor waited till everyone had spoken then he outlined what we would be studying. He gave us the first chapter in the textbook to read and told us we would discuss it in the next class. Afterward I made my way to my next class, wondering what I should say if this happened again in another class. I heard some laughter behind me and found a group of five or six boys walking behind me. One of them called out to me, "You married?" I retorted with a resounding "No" and they laughed even louder. They were holding something up and waving it at me. As they got closer I realized it was a condom, I figured that my statement in class would have repercussions, but I was mortified. I found my room as quickly as I could and made sure to sit farther back so I would have time to think. This was not the warm, forgiving atmosphere of church and my new family, but a foreign, judgmental, harassing one I was not used to. My thoughts went immediately to my childhood and I was nervous and scared.

English class was quite different. No one was singled out and the professor was very clear about what she expected. It gave me time to recover my composure and then I was free for lunch. Mom had packed a lunch for me so I made my way to the dining hall and found a seat at a table along the side of the hall. I had just sat down when this guy came over and asked me if this was my first year. I reluctantly answered, even though I simply wished in my heart he would go away. Then a couple of girls came over and asked if they could join us. They told us their names were Susan and Chloe. The guy said his name was Devon. I opened up a bit and told them my name was Lillian. We chatted about the university and Chloe offered to show us around so we would know where everything was. At the end of the tour, Chloe asked if we could meet again the next day at the same spot.

I was much happier then and resolved to be more courageous when I attended Algebra class after lunch. Susan had told me at lunch that she was taking Algebra, and I was glad to see her come through the classroom door. Her presence boosted my courage and I became less nervous, knowing that she would be there. It was unbelievable, really, because we had just met. I had known her for an hour but her friendliness at lunch made all the difference in my perspective of college life. My last class that day was my elective choice and I had chosen to do Home Economics. I figured that as a single mother I would need to have a grasp of how to run a home and manage the budget and so on. I was not disappointed and it just added to my enjoyment of the day. The teacher was sweet and spent the time giving us a rundown on how our time would be spent. Tuesdays would be mostly book work with homework for the following Tuesday, and Thursdays would be practical work. I figured I would enjoy this class and learn important lessons for my future.

I was glad to be home at the end of that day. Everyone wanted to know how my day had gone and I told them I had met some new friends. Mom was happy and told me Bobby had been very good. He had taken the bottle well and had taken his nap after about 30 minutes of fighting sleep. I expected that because he had always fallen asleep in my arms. I realized I would have to teach him how to fall asleep on his own. That first night was easy. We played a little before he started to eat and then I tried to keep him awake while he was eating. He just wanted to fall asleep. I kept talking to him and he would open his eyes and grin at me. He was so happy to see me. When he had finished eating I dressed him for bed, something I had always done before feeding him. Then I laid him in his crib and sat beside the crib reading a story from one of his little books. It worked well and he was soon asleep. Then I started on my homework. There was a lot to take in as I did the reading for Government. I didn't know if the professor would test us on the reading so I read slowly and tried to absorb the information. I did my Algebra next and finished it in record time. Then I read my English assignment. I had made up my mind that schoolwork should never interfere with my daily reading of the Bible so I took the time to read a couple of chapters. I was reading in Luke and when I read how people criticized the lord Jesus because he was eating with people, it made me feel better about what had happened that morning. I decided I would not tell Mom and the others about that incident with the boys making fun of me, because they would only worry. I knew I was going to be all right. I spent an hour with Mom and Sharen before going to bed. As I thought about my life, I thanked God again for giving me these dear friends, a place to live, and the ability to go to school.

As I drifted off to sleep I thought about what direction to go. I had thought at one time of being a doctor or a nurse. There were so many options open to me now that I allowed my mind to wander. What about a teacher? Then I would be able to help Bobby when he grew up and started school. The more I thought about it the more I liked the idea. I didn't need to change anything because most of my classes were general education this semester. I settled into a peaceful sleep and awoke the next morning before my alarm well rested and refreshed and ready to face the world—the world of college, that is.

My second day was much easier and I had less misgivings about Bobby. I knew he was happy with his nana and auntie, and I knew he was loved. That was all that mattered. That day I had Economics, History, and in the afternoon English Literature. I was in seventh heaven because I loved all three and had excelled in school in these subjects. I did not see those horrible boys and I met my new friends in the lunchroom again. Mom was picking me up and class ended early, so I did a quick trip to the office to see what subjects I would need for teaching. The office staff pointed me in the right direction for the information I needed and I wrote down everything. When I went out to meet Mom and Bobby, I told them I had finally made up my mind what I was going to study for. I was going to be a teacher. Mom was thrilled. She thought it would give me a better work timetable than a nurse's schedule and when I thought about it I agreed.

Wednesday came and Government class along with it. I was dreading going back. On the way, Mom told me she had prayed that morning for strength for me as I faced all the new people and ideas, wisdom to know when to confront and when to be silent, and courage to stand up for my Lord and my convictions. I thanked her and thought about those things as I walked to the lecture hall. It occurred to me I had not told anyone the previous day that I was a Christian. I determined that I would at least tell my lunchroom friends that I was a Christian. We had to sit in our assigned seats in the lecture hall and there was no way I could change, so I gritted my teeth and told myself several times I had nothing to be ashamed of. There was an empty seat on the other side of the aisle from me and before the lecture got started, a counselor came in and momentarily spoke with the professor. He nodded agreement with what she was asking him and went to the door and ushered in Devon. He took the empty seat and nodded to me. The professor made some statements about our reading assignment and then asked random students what they thought about various parts of the assignment. I was one of the first and he entered into a discussion with me when I gave my answer. Then he asked one of the boys and was not happy with his answer at all. He then asked this boy if he had read the assignment and after giving several excuses he admitted that he had not. He was told to write an essay on part of the assignment and be warned that all assignments are required to be done. I found myself slipping back into gloating mode, thinking he had that coming. I turned to look at Devon and saw a sad look on his face as if he felt sorry for the guy. I was reprimanded in my soul and realized that the way I was feeling was not glorifying to God. At the end of the lecture Devon asked where my next class was and said that he would see me at lunch. It was enough to get me away from the lecture hall and away from those boys who had been so mean.

Lunchtime seemed to come very quickly. Susan ate quickly and had to leave to do an errand. I took a deep breath and said, "I am very glad you made friends with me and I hope we can be really good friends but I just want you to know from the start that I am a Christian." I didn't know where to go from there so I just stopped. Devon was the first to speak, and he told us he was also a Christian and he was glad I had the courage to tell us because he had wanted to but was not sure how to bring it up. Chloe was grinning from ear to ear as she told us her parents had prayed with her that morning and asked God to direct her to friends who shared her faith. She said she couldn't wait to tell them that God had already answered their prayers before they even asked. I felt very emotional so I could not speak for a few minutes as I contemplated God's goodness. There was just no end to his blessings. I remembered a verse which Mom had told me one day: "God is able to do exceeding abundantly above all that we ask or think. God not only gave His only Son to die in our stead but he takes care of all the little things in life as well."

When I found my voice I asked Devon what he thought of the professor's treatment of the guy in our class. He said he was acquainted with the boy and he needed prayer. He thought the professor was right in what he did because the boy needed strong guidance; nevertheless, he felt sorry he had been humiliated. I realized I had not even thought of praying for those boys because I was so angry with them. I had so much to learn about the Christian life. I had been given so much and yet I did not seem to know when to give back.

I thought about my Dad and silently told God I had forgiven him and the boys. I felt as if a burden had been lifted from my shoulders. Chloe asked what church we went to because she was new to the area and had not found a church home yet. I told her the name of the church I was going to and invited her to come along. Devon said the church he belonged to was not in the area and he traveled quite a distance each day. He was looking for somewhere to live but in the meantime, he was commuting. That afternoon as we left Algebra, Susan turned to me and asked, "Do you pray?" I told her I did and she asked me to pray because something had come up and she didn't know if she was going to be able to continue with her classes. I prayed silently as we walked and squeezed her hand when we parted. I was so excited when I saw Mom that afternoon. I told her what I had done and then what had happened and she just smiled. I knew then that everything would be all right.

Bobby's birthday was the best. He was so happy with so many kids around. They were so good with him, I thought because they were happy too. I couldn't help but compare my new family with the one I was born into. I thought of my little sister and hoped she was happy. The first few months of college went quickly. Chloe, Susan, Devon, and I became firm friends and I was able to keep up with my studies. Chloe and her brother and parents started attending church with us. Devon was still commuting. Bobby was growing like a weed and was always happy and bubbling with excitement. He had adjusted to my absence very well. My body had adjusted well too and I was able to continue breastfeeding Bobby and expressing milk for when I was gone. Everything was going smoothly. Life at home was wonderful, and being part of a large family was the best. Sharen received joyful news that her husband was coming home for Thanksgiving. He was not going to be home for Christmas but everyone was glad he would be home at all. The preparations for Thanksgiving started and everyone had a part to play. We talked about the menu, the seating arrangements, and the decorations. Sharen included us in everything, and I enjoyed the camaraderie of having a big sister. Her children were wonderful with Bobby, playing with him and including him as much as they could. He had started walking and was into everything. Sharen was taking two units at the university so she went there every day for her class. It was in the middle of the day so she was always home before Mom came to pick me up. Life was good. I realized there was no need for me to worry about anything. The pastor was right: God had everything under control. I had a church home, I was going to university, my son couldn't be happier, and I couldn't be happier. I had Christian friends at school and a home where I was loved beyond measure. It was hard to imagine what my life would have been like without the Lord and without the help of those who loved him. It seemed a long time ago that I walked into that little café and met my guardian angel in the person of Mrs. Alford.

Chapter 8

THANKSGIVING WAS EVEN BETTER THAN I COULD have wished. Sharen's husband arrived two days before and joined in the cooking and preparations. Sharen had asked me if I had any friends from school who had nowhere to go for Thanksgiving so I had asked Susan and Devon what they were doing. Sharen had already asked Chloe's family to come. Susan started crying and Devon said he was going to be at home. I had been praying for Susan every day but she had not brought the subject up so neither had I. She was still coming to class so I thought everything had been resolved. Later we were on our way to the library, so I took her hand and asked if everything was all right. She shook her head. She didn't explain why, or say anything at all until we sat down at the table. We chose a table in the corner so she could talk if she wanted to. She told me her Mom had been having tests done and they were not looking good. I felt so sad for her. She said she felt as if she could not go on. She loved her Mom very much and depended on her for so much, and she was worried she was going to die. I hugged her and told her I was sorry and if I could help I would. She said that no one could help because no one could understand what she was going through. I knew she was feeling sorry for herself as well as being scared of her mom's health problems.

I felt led to tell her my story. She listened with eyes wide open and when I told her my mother had died she became upset and accused me of making up stories.

"Your Mom is very much alive!" she exclaimed.

I realized how confused she was and continued telling her my story. She calmed down and listened intently. When I got to the part about being pregnant, she gasped and asked me if I had had an abortion. I told her I had not, that I had a wonderful little boy called Bobby, and that God had worked out my whole life for me. I confessed I had been where she was, confused and feeling alone, but God had taken care of me and not only saved my life but saved my soul. I told her that I felt sure God had a purpose for her and she should lean on him and not fall into Satan's trap of despair. She thanked me for sharing and then we had to run to class. I didn't see her until after Thanksgiving but thought about her often during that time and prayed for her.

We were having quite a crowd. Sharen's mom and sister were arriving for Thanksgiving. They were staying in a nearby hotel for a day or two, and I was so glad to see them again. Chloe and her family were arriving in time for dinner. It was so much fun, having that many people all in the same place. I so loved being part of a large family. Bobby's happiness was obvious and when he giggled everyone laughed with him. In my heart I thanked God for allowing him to be a part of a loving family. That started me thinking about my birth family. I wondered about Bobby, Joseph, and Thomas. Most of all I wondered about my little sister Ruthie. I wondered if she ever thought about me. I wondered if God had protected her and given her a loving family. I resolved I would try to find her and make sure she was safe.

When we sat down to dinner, Sharen's husband prayed and asked God to bless all those present and all those who were in our thoughts at that time. After the prayer he said he was so very thankful for his family and friends and for being alive. I noticed Sharen stealing a glance at him but he said no more except to ask if anyone else would like to share what they were thankful for. Mom was the first to speak and she said that she was thankful for God's provision for her. She said she had envisioned a lonely existence but God had provided her with a daughter, a lifelong wish on her part, and a loving family who cared for her, and she couldn't wish for more. At first I was confused, not realizing she was calling me her daughter, and then I was overcome with the love this sweet lady had for me. Sharen said how glad she was to have her husband home safe and sound. Grace said she had so many things to be thankful for that it would take all day and we needed to eat before the meal got cold. I looked around and there were quite a few tear-filled eyes, and I knew she was being kind not selfish. Sharen got up and hugged her and told everyone to help themselves to whatever they liked. The food was beyond scrumptious. She had done something with the green beans, which were never a favorite of mine, and even they were delicious. When the meal was over, Grace and Mom retired to the kitchen and shooed everyone out. I noticed that Sharen and her husband took off, rather quickly, by themselves. I sensed that there was something being left unsaid but had no idea what. I watched as Bobby played with the other children, and then Chloe and I got to sit together and she told me how glad she was I had invited her family to church. They were all happy there and loved the people. She asked if I knew what was going on with Susan and I told her that her Mom was ill and was having some tests done.

Then she asked about Bobby. Since I had told Susan my story I felt I should tell Chloe also. I asked her if she wanted to hear the short version or the long version. She laughed and said that we were on school break so she would take the long version. She cried when I told her of my family, she was horrified when I told her that my mother had died, and she sympathized when I told her how my sister and brother and I were split up and I had never seen my sister again. She asked if I had seen my brother, and I shamefacedly told her how I had turned my back on him. She shuddered when I got to the rape and what happened with my foster family. I told her about meeting Mom and how she had taken me in and loved me and Bobby like a true mother. She hugged me and reminded me that God is good, no matter what the circumstance or situation. She thanked me for sharing and we linked pinkies and said, "Friends for life." I realized Bobby was standing at my knee looking quizzically at me. I swept him up and he kissed me repeatedly, as if he knew what I had been through. I told him nothing like that would ever happen to him, as if he knew what any of it meant. It was actually a great relief to me to be able to share with someone. I guessed I would have to tell Devon one day too.

One of Sharen's kids wanted us to play some games so off we went to the family room and the conversation became lighter for the rest of the day. Sharen was missing for a while and I noticed Grace hugging her and wondered what was going on. Soon it was time for snacks and the time passed quickly. Chloe's parents decided it was time to go around eight o'clock and I got Bobby settled in bed. He was asleep very quickly. Mom and I were cleaning up in the kitchen and I asked her if she knew what was up. She said Steve had been involved in a serious accident and two people had died. It was not his fault and one of the people who had since died had been drunk, but he was pretty shook up and was going to take some time off before going back. Time is short. In the blink of an eye, life could be over. He felt as if God had protected him and one of the paramedics told him he was lucky to be alive and to be able to walk away from that crash. Mom reminded me that if I wanted to change anything in my life I needed to do it soon. I told her I had made up my mind to search for my little sister. She was happy to hear that and asked, "And your Dad?" I told her that I would try to find him too, but my sister was first.

The following day was bittersweet. Everyone was packing up to go home and saying their goodbyes. We tried to do some cleaning up, but those who were leaving wanted to talk and catch up with everything. Before we knew it, the day was almost over. Everyone left before supper, and we sat down to a delicious meal of leftovers. After Mom and I cleared away the food and dishes we played with Bobby for a little while before he went off to bed. He was asleep in no time because he had had no nap in the afternoon. He had so enjoyed playing with everyone. I thanked my heavenly Father for taking care of us in such a wonderful way. It is true: his grace is sufficient.

Saturday dawned and Bobby and I were up bright and early. After breakfast the other kids captured his attention and I tried to figure out how I should go about finding my sister. Mom said I should call the welfare office and ask them for help. I tried but of course it was Saturday and the office was closed. I did not leave a message but wrote down the numbers on the answering machine recording. I was excited and terrified at the same time. What if she was dead? What if she would never forgive me?

Sunday was wonderful. Pastor brought us a message from 2 Timothy, Chapter 2. We were reminded that God knows those who are his. What a wonderful truth that is. All that time when I worried and tried to fit in with my foster family, all the time at home when my Dad scared me so much, God knew me and was molding me for his purpose. I felt so blessed and humbled. The pastor went on to remind us that some people are given lofty jobs to do, like be the governor or the president, but some are given lowly jobs to do like be the janitor in a school or hospital. All of these jobs are God-directed and should be carried out for his glory. He reminded us of the scripture that says, "It is better to be a doorkeeper in the House of God than to dwell in the tents of wickedness. "We are to follow after righteousness, faith, charity, and peace." Those were big goals. I was trying to do the right thing, but did I exercise faith? Even as the question came into my mind, Pastor said that even if we have faith the size of a mustard seed, it pleases God. Verse 23 was very meaningful to me also. In college, there were those who would ask silly questions like how many angels can sit on a pinhead. I realized it was useless to enter into discussions like these when the time could be better spent declaring what God had done for his people. My mind was running in many different directions on the way home; Mom sensed that and was very quiet, keeping Bobby entertained.

We talked later in the afternoon and I had so many questions to ask her. I asked her about the striving and she said it meant rendering strife and making unnecessary problems. I wondered about my father and how he was always picking fights with my brothers and my mother. I asked if she thought God would ever forgive someone who created that kind of strife. She told me, as she had done many times before, that God has his people and no matter what they have done, he will draw them to himself and forgive them through the cross work of the Lord Jesus. She told me I am only responsible for my own behavior and that the end of the verse was just as important as the beginning. I read the verse again: "Be gentle unto all men, apt to teach and patient." Mom said that disobeying the second part part was just as bad as disobeying the first part. God wants us to be the bearers of the good news of the gospel and teach others that God sent his only son into the world to be born of a woman, to suffer the indignities of being a human child, fully dependent on someone else for care even though he was the king of Heaven; to suffer the indignities of torture and hanging by evil men who were ruled by Satan; to suffer the anguish of being forsaken by his father in that instant of death; to lie in a borrowed tomb because his family were so poor they didn't have anywhere to bury him; and to rise again triumphantly, defeating Satan, defeating death, and gaining the victory for those who believe in him. I understood, finally. God had saved me for a purpose and I needed to seek his face to find out what that purpose was. We prayed together and I was so thankful for the fact that he had not only provided me with a home and family, but had fulfilled all my needs, including spiritual needs, and I felt I could do no other but serve him.

The next few weeks were busy as tests and exams loomed over us. There was much reading to be done. There were dental appointments and checkups for Bobby, who was doing great according to his doctor. I did manage to talk to someone in the welfare office who gave me a number to call. It was Child Protective Services and I called them. The guy who answered the phone had never heard of our family, but said he would look into the matter and get back to me. Mom told me to be patient, not to stress but to keep trying. It is difficult to be patient when you set your mind on something and just seem to meet with brick walls. I also had to figure out what to give to everyone for Christmas. I liked working with paper and Sharen had a machine which laminated, so I decided I would make everyone a bookmark individualized with their names and something they were interested in.

I had forgotten that I was waiting for a phone call when one day I received a call from a social worker who told me she had known my sister and had an address for me. I was excited and terrified all over again. She did not have a telephone number and we had no idea where the address was. Sharen's husband was packed and ready to leave again, but he took the time to find a telephone number for that address. I called the number thinking I was not going to be able to speak if anyone answered. A woman answered and I told her my name and that I was looking for my sister Ruth. She said she did not know anybody called Ruth. I told her she had been in foster care and the social worker had given me her address. She started yelling at me and saying she didn't know anybody like that. I was shaking but managed to say I was sorry for disturbing her. Mom and I prayed together and asked God to please help us to find Ruth. I blamed myself for leaving it so long. Then I thought Bobby might have found her because he would have looked for her a long time ago. Mom said it was just another brick wall to be climbed. In my heart I knew God would take care of her, After all, he had taken care of me.

Christmas came and we had a wonderful time together. Sharen's mom and sister came the day after Christmas. I know Sharen missed her husband but she busied herself with cooking and talking. She did get to talk with him for five minutes on the phone and we all hardly breathed so she could hear. Even Bobby was quiet. I understood what it was like not to be near someone you loved at Christmas. I made a pact with myself to try again to find Ruth in the new year.

Christmas break was over fast and I was back in class. My results were in and I was pleased with them. Mom took us for ice cream to celebrate. We laughed at Bobby. He had ice cream on his nose and chin and everywhere. I just let him have fun. It didn't seem to matter because he was so happy. I loved to hear him giggle. I talked to Mom about getting a job to help with expenses and she said she had no problem so long as I didn't let my studies suffer. I had noticed a sign posted on the library door for a 5:00 p.m. to 8:00 p.m. position Monday through Friday. It was a lot and I wouldn't be home for Bobby. I wasn't sure if I would have time to study. I ended up applying and then discovered that Chloe had applied as well. We were both asked for an interview and she was first. She said she would wait for me. During my interview the librarian, Miss Turner, indicated she was going to hire me because of my experience at the café. I felt sorry for Chloe and as Miss Turner was shaking my hand I asked her if we could share the job. She told me to sit down and asked me how that would work. I said we could work every other week or every other day. She thought about that for a minute and then said that as Mondays were usually busy she had thought of having an extra person that day, so if we could both work Mondays and divide the other days she would do it. I brought Chloe in and we decided I would work Monday, Tuesday, and Thursday, and she would work Monday, Wednesday, and Friday.

We were to start the following week. Mom was glad it wasn't going to be every day, and I was glad too for Bobby's sake. We worked out a schedule for Bobby so Mom would have some time to herself. She said she didn't care about free time and that she loved watching Bobby. I just didn't want her to ever think I was taking advantage of her when I could do things myself.

Pastor asked for prayer requests often and I never spoke out with mine. He looked directly at me one morning and I mentioned that Devon, a friend of mine, needed to find an inexpensive place near the university so he would not have to commute. He smiled as he added that to his list of requests. Later as we were leaving he asked what kind of lodging Devon was looking for. I told him he really needed to room with some other boys because the apartment rents were too high for his budget. He said he would look into it and asked for his telephone number. I didn't think any more about it until one lunchtime Devon said he'd had a call from the pastor and he was going to meet with him that day after classes. He asked me how he knew and I told him I had asked the pastor to add it to the church's prayer request list. He thanked me and said he had not received any details about but was really happy because the gas money and the commute were getting tiresome He also whispered in my ear that he and his family had been praying about it too because it would mean he could spend more time with me. I blushed when I thought of what the implications of that were. Next day at lunch he told us he was moving in with a couple from the church. They had a granny flat at the back of their home in which the guy's mother had lived. She had been in an assisted living facility for some time and had told them to use it for whatever they needed. They had spoken to the pastor about it the day before I had asked for prayer, and asked him if he knew anybody who needed a place to live. They had specifically asked if he knew any college students because they wanted to use it to help someone. It was amazing, and I was reminded once again of God's providence. He was talking to Mom when she came to meet me after classes and she told me he had invited us over to see his new place. He also told her he would be able to bring me home so she wouldn't have to do that anymore. Mom was grinning from ear to ear but made no remarks about him. She followed him to the flat and realized we had eaten in that home a few times. The flat was out back and was really nice. There was a bedroom, bathroom and kitchen. There was a bed and dresser in the bedroom, a table and chairs, and a couch and easy chair in the other room. There was a refrigerator, an oven, and a microwave. He was able to use the washing machine and dryer in the garage so he had everything he needed. Devon was thrilled. He said his mom was already packing bedclothes and dishes. He said she had always worried about him driving when he was tired and was glad he had found somewhere to live. He left to go home with a big grin on his face and said he would see us the next day.

He moved in the following weekend. He wanted Mom and me to help him, even though his Mom had come as well. She had brought enough food to feed an army and said it would probably be gone in a week. She had brought sandwiches and fruit for our lunch and she and Mom talked endlessly about boys and their foibles. She kneeled down on the floor and talked to Bobby and he showed her his latest treasure: a picture box with knobs he turned to move the picture. We were all done around three o'clock and Devon and his Mom left to go home. On the way home Mom asked me about Devon. She said she believed he was a nice young man. I was nervous because his Mom seemed to know all about me. He seemed so comfortable with me in his flat and his Mom acted like I was supposed to be there. I wasn't sure what to think.

We were sitting in church on Sunday morning, trying to get Bobby settled before Pastor came in when, much to my surprise, Devon slipped quietly into the seat beside me. I looked at Mom and she just smiled and kept her attention on Bobby. Devon was attentive to the sermon, and sang the hymns with gusto. I kept stealing a glance at him every so often, but he was paying close attention to what the pastor was saying. Afterwards as we were leaving, a family from the church invited us to their home for a meal and asked if this was my young man. I was embarrassed and didn't answer. Devon tried to cover for me by saying he had just moved to the area so he could be near the university. They invited him along too and we had a cordial afternoon. Bobby was the center of attraction which kept the focus off me, and I was able to regain my composure. Devon thanked the host very much and left saying he had some things to take care of before the evening service. He told me he would see me later. I asked Mom what I should do if anybody else asked me a question like that, and she told me to stop stressing and just let things happen the way they are supposed to. I hoped no one else would ask. I liked Devon but wasn't sure how he felt.

Mom said she would stay home with Bobby and that I should go with Sharen. Before it was time to leave there was a knock at the door and Devon was there asking if I would ride with him to church. Sharen diplomatically said that would work out great because she needed to stay behind for a short committee meeting. I took a deep breath and went with Devon. I had always been comfortable with him before and could not understand my discomfort at this time. He kept looking at me but I couldn't meet his eye. He parked the car and as we were a little early he asked if we could talk. He had sensed my uneasiness and wanted to clear up any misunderstanding. He told me he loved being with me and did not want to cause any discomfort. He told me I should not feel obligated to help him or ride with him if I did not want to. He said he realized we had three more years of school which we both needed to concentrate on, so he did not want to put any pressure on me romantically because he never wanted to lose me as a friend. I had been staring in front of me because I didn't know what he wanted to talk about. I turned and looked at him when I heard a quiver in his voice and realized he was near to tears. I told him I did want to spend time with him and ride with him, but I didn't know what he would think about people calling him my young man when he wasn't. He heaved a sigh of relief, I think wiped a tear from his eye, and said he would be thrilled to be called my young man by anyone. Whew! I let out a long breath. I guess I'd been holding my breath, but now I felt as if the tension was gone and I was able to relax again. He asked me if he could kiss me on the cheek and I agreed. Then he surprised me and told me he intended to marry me one day. We went into the service feeling like our normal selves again, and even looked at one another and grinned a few times before it was over. On the way out Pastor asked him if he was happy with his new abode and he grabbed Pastor's hand and shook it warmly, saying he was more than pleased because it was an answer to his prayer. Pastor grinned at me but said nothing and I was glad. Being the soul of discretion, he has never spoken the words that were on his tongue that day.

Chapter 9

FIVE YEARS LATER

GOD'S BLESSINGS ARE INNUMERABLE. I NEVER CEASED to be in awe of God's plan for my life. I thought about the day I walked down the street from my foster parents' home, forsaken by everyone I knew, pregnant from rape, and with nowhere to live. All my possessions were in a plastic bag. I was lost but God, in his infinite love, scooped me up and gave me a home and family who loved me unconditionally. Now I had graduated from university, had no debt (another miracle), and was about to start a new job teaching in a Christian school very close to where my Mom had lived. I had just completed my year of teacher training in the same school where Bobby attended kindergarten. My new job was teaching first grade and Bobby would be in my class. That would make it so much easier for him to settle into his new surroundings and life. Devon had a degree in engineering and had secured a position in a college not too far from where Mom had lived. We were moving back to Mom's house that summer, but not before Devon and I were to be married. Sharen's husband was home for good. He had gone back to his old job and although at times he was very quiet, he seemed to have escaped major problems even though he admitted to us he had been in the war zone. He had never told Sharen the whole truth about where he was, and how much danger he had been in. We found out he was flying helicopters into the war zone to pick up injured soldiers and Marines. It gave us all cold chills but he reminded us that he was home and he was well and that God had been with him the whole time. Now the conflict was over and he was back home with his loved ones. Everything had worked out for everyone. My joy was marred for a little while when Mom decided we should live in her home and she would find somewhere else to live. I couldn't believe she did not want to live with us. I had always assumed that she would. I told Devon how disappointed I was and he said he would talk to her. She told him we needed some time to ourselves and we shouldn't worry about her. I was so proud of Devon when he told me he told her he refused to live in her home if she didn't. He told her she was very precious to both of us and we needed her. She had wavered a little but when he told her Bobby would be so upset if she wasn't there anymore he would feel abandoned, and that did it. She said of course she would live with us. I hugged him; he always knew the right thing to say.

Mom decided she would stay with Sharen until September and move back for the start of school. That would give us time to get acquainted with the house and everything before she arrived. She also asked Bobby if he would stay with her so she wouldn't get lonely in the meantime. I knew she was making sure we had our honeymoon time even though we had opted to forgo that detail. Always the loving mother, always thoughtful, she was indeed an abundant blessing in my life. Sharen's husband had been home for a while, and he and Devon got along famously. Sharen worked feverishly beside me, helping with all the preparations for the wedding. It was going to be on Saturday in the second week of June. Mom and I had been working on my dress every spare moment when Devon was busy with something. We trained the kids to be guards, so if Devon appeared they would let us know and waylay him so we could get it out of sight. It was all so much fun. It was like a game to them and I was thrilled they were all a part of it. They were all taking part in the ceremony so everyone was excited. One of my friends from church was making the cake, or cakes as it turned out. Chloe was decorating the church and the church ladies were providing the meal. Jo Ann, who seemed to be in charge of the church ladies, told me there was to be a surprise after the meal was over and we were not to be planning a quick getaway. I didn't know what that was going to be but because of her fun-loving personality, I knew it would be enjoyable. We were not in a hurry anyway as we were not traveling far. We were going to go to our new home.

Chapter 10

*A*T LAST THE DAY WAS HERE. BOBBY WAS FLYING everywhere, knocking things over. Everybody was going in different directions, misplacing things, and spilling drinks too near special dresses. You would have thought Sharen was getting married or Mom for that matter. My mind was racing from one thing to another. Had I packed everything? Would I be a good wife? Will Devon get there in time? Will Bobby behave during the ceremony? Will the sun stay out for the photographs? Mom, as usual, knew I was getting stressed and she ushered me into the bedroom and held me tight. She told me to stop thinking and let God. It was a saying she had said to me very often, but instead of saying give it up and let go she would say give it up and let God. She guided me to the side of the bed and I sat down. She sat down beside me and prayed for stillness in my heart and comfort in my soul. Then she told me to breathe, and I inhaled deeply. I felt the anxiety leave me and from that moment on I enjoyed every minute of my day.

And what a day it was. Mark, one of the members of the church, owned a car rental company. JoAnn had talked him into loaning us a rather expensive car for free. The only stipulation was that he would drive. When everyone walked out the door to drive to the church and I was on my own, I looked at myself in the mirror one more time and prayed audibly, and thanked God for his unbelievable blessings. It wasn't long until Mark arrived and ushered me into his gray and white convertible. I was a bit dismayed at first but he put the cover up as soon as he climbed into the car. It was not far to the church and when we arrived the cover went down again for reasons which were very obvious. There were dozens of people all taking photos and grinning widely. When Mark helped me from the car, Steve, who was going to be giving me away, appeared out of the crowd and escorted me to the foyer of the church. I felt like I was watching instead of participating. It was all somewhat surreal. I stepped inside the sanctuary and saw Devon waiting for me with a look of awe on his face. *I had not disappointed him*, I thought. I felt as if I was walking on air as I followed Bobby and all of Sharen's children down the aisle. Bobby kept looking back at me, and I couldn't tell if he wasn't sure I was his mother or if he just needed reassurance. That was all I needed to forget my nervousness, and I smiled at him. He responded immediately, and grinned from ear to ear, then walked proudly to the front of the church. When I reached the front, Devon stepped in beside me and Steve sat down. The pastor introduced us to the congregation and proceeded with the ceremony. "This is a Christian wedding," he said with a smile on his face. I enjoyed every minute of the day after that. Pastor reminded us that the Lord Jesus went to at least one wedding when he was here on earth and he was most certainly attending this one. He said some very kind things about both of us, and then invited everyone present to attend the reception afterward.

The church ladies had accomplished the unbelievable: the church hall was truly beautiful, with lace and greenery on all the windows, an archway over the table at the front where the wedding party sat, and the tables all covered with white tablecloths and greenery and yellow roses to match my bouquet. I had requested yellow roses for my bouquet because someone once told me that yellow roses reminded them of their loved ones. I wished I had found my sister before this day but did not, so the yellow roses were for her. The meal was delicious and everyone was so happy. I didn't really want to leave, but the time came for me to say goodbye to my dear Mom and Sharen, her children, Steve, and the hardest of all, my sweet Bobby. I had tears in my eyes as we drove off, and I was deep in thought when Devon offered me a penny for them. I asked him to repeat what he had said and he told me that he had offered a penny for my thoughts and added he hoped I was not having second thoughts. I told him that I had never been so happy, that I couldn't believe that God could have changed my life so much. He asked me what I would like to do the rest of the day, and we agreed to go home and change, get a picnic together, and go to the lake for a while. When we arrived home that night, we were so tired, but both agreed that the day could not have been more wonderful. We had prayer together and Devon read the Bible reading for the day. Afterward he told me that he would make it one of his priorities to find my sister. I knew he would. The following day, we rose early and unpacked the trunk of the car. Mom and Sharen had packed it for us. We found two hampers of food for the refrigerator and enough groceries to last the two weeks. They had all kinds of snacks and drinks. There was also a box of cleaning materials to clean up the dusty house. We had a quick breakfast and set off for church. I was so looking forward to seeing my friends again. Everybody was so kind and many had gifts for us because Mom had told them we were coming home.

The pastor preached a message from 1 Peter, Chapter 3, verses 1-7. He reminded us that marriage is a God-ordained relationship between a man and a woman. Wives are to submit to and love their husbands. Husbands are to love and cherish their wives just like Christ loved his church. That meant they were not to be bullies and try to humiliate their wives in any way. Instead they should teach each other in humility. He reminded us that women are not inferior to men, just different. Women have the unique task of growing the next generation of divinely-created souls. This task is entrusted to them by the Almighty God. God had ordained this to be so. He told us mankind has rejected God's plan and decided they will change things around. They make drugs and do surgeries which change the appearance of men and women, and they make drugs and do surgeries to kill the babies while they are in the safe wombs. They decide they know better than God. Men have perverted sex with men and women do the same. Some have even had sex with animals. There is no end to the lengths Satan will go to try to subvert the beautiful relationship which God ordained. He expected a man to marry a woman and stay with her as long as she lived. Now lawyers make a lot of money fighting legal battles between men and women who no longer want to do that. There are many in the world who have rejected God's law and that is why there is chaos. Pastor then went in a different direction and reiterated his instruction to men to love their wives, honor them, and give them their place in the family unit. The husband is not the slave owner, so he should consider his wife in all their decisions. Remember God has instructed men to leave their own parents and start a new family with his wife. She is the one God-chosen to grow those which he creates in her womb, with men as their protectors. Men are the people God chose to be stronger and more powerful and women are their helpers. God's plan is so wonderful when people stick to it, but when they transgress, all they have is chaos and confusion. Pastor then encouraged us to serve him in everything we do, love him and obey his commands, love one another, and be blessed by him.

Afterward the church had prepared a meal for everyone, but most were subdued as we contemplated what we had just heard. Afterward I offered to help clean up but the ladies told me that as I was a guest I should just mingle and get reacquainted. There were several new people and we were introduced to them. Devon kept looking for an opportunity to talk to the pastor, who seemed to be very busy counseling different members. I asked him on the way home what he wanted to see the pastor about. He said he wanted to talk to him about church membership. I was overjoyed and thanked God one more time for giving me this man to love. We spent the rest of the day planning our next two weeks and making lists of things we needed to do and things we needed to buy.

We set to the following morning, and dusted and cleaned, then we went for a drive and I showed Devon where my high school was, where the park was, where the stores were, and where the church was. We went to the little café where I had worked all those years ago, and the owner was so glad to see me. He made us a wonderful meal on the house and sat and talked for quite a while. When we arrived home we moved furniture around, and made the room, which had been for storage mostly, into a bedroom for Bobby. We decided we would go sightseeing the whole next day and do some shopping as well.

There were several changes Devon wanted to do to make things more comfortable for Mom, who had instructed us to move her things into my old room so that we could use her larger room. It had the bathroom and an adjacent dressing room which we could use as a study or workroom. While driving around, we found ourselves in the district where I used to live. I showed Devon our old home and the school I had attended. Those were bittersweet memories. I caught sight of the hardware store that Bobby had worked in and pointed it out. Devon said he could probably find what he needed in there, so we parked and went inside.

The young man greeted us as we entered the store, told us his name was Matthew, and asked us what we needed. Devon stopped to talk to him and explain what he wanted to do. Matthew came out from behind the counter and walked with Devon to fetch the items required. I just stood by the counter, waiting, and wondering if the same guy who employed Bobby would still be there. There was an office window at the other side of the store and someone inside waved. I nodded, thinking it might be him and maybe he would know where Bobby was. As I contemplated asking him if he had any news of Bobby, he came out to see if I needed anything. I told him my husband was shopping. He looked at me intently and I sensed something about him, something familiar. It was dark in that area of the store and the light was on behind him in the office. He came closer and said, "Lillian?" I could hardly breathe. Tears welled up in my eyes. I couldn't move. I just did not believe this man was my long-lost brother. He ran the last few steps and gathered me up in his arms and hugged me so hard I thought I would die. He was crying. Neither of us could speak. The embrace was suddenly interrupted by Devon, who had just emerged from the back of the store. He was furious and asked what Bobby thought he was doing. I told him this was my brother and suddenly all of us were talking at the same time and Matthew looked on in bewilderment.

Bobby explained to him he had lost track of me a long time ago and I was the Lillian whom they had been praying about. He joined in the excitement then and told me Pastor Bob had prayed for me every week ever since he had known him. Bobby then told Matthew he was going to leave, that three other employees were coming at eleven, and that he would come back if he was needed in the meantime. He made a phone call and then told us to follow him in the car. We did and he stopped at a huge, beautiful home and actually ran from the car to the front door, not waiting for us. I was asking myself why he had brought us here. He rang the doorbell and waved for us to follow him. When we did, there was my friend Anna, who nearly knocked me down, when she scooted past Bobby and hugged me. She was pregnant so my mind was racing.

"You are married?" I questioned. She laughed and looked at Bobby. Then she ushered us into the most beautiful room I have ever seen, and there sat a woman in a wheelchair who was weeping. Bobby told me that this lady was my grandmother. I was totally confused, as I thought they had been killed before any of us were born.

"This is Dad's mom," said Bobby.

I was in total shock and Devon was having difficulty taking it all in. After hugs all around, Devon finally said, "I have never seen God work so fast. We were praying this morning that you would find some of your family and before the day is ended he has done just that. It really gives me more faith to believe that he will help us find your sister."

Bobby started to laugh and Anna and my grandmother joined in. I was so emotional and I didn't understand why they were laughing. I broke down in tears. Devon asked them why they were laughing, and I could tell he was upset with them. Bobby quickly apologized and told us to come with him. We were bewildered but we followed him to the car. He drove us to a large building and he motioned us inside. It was obvious he was enjoying himself. He ran over to reception and spoke to the woman at the desk. She ran to the elevator and disappeared. We stood there just looking at each other and then at Bobby, still not believing he was standing there with us.

I pinched myself in case it was a dream. The door of the elevator opened and there stood the receptionist with another young woman. They walked towards us and I felt faint because there in front of me stood a grown-up version of my little Ruthie. She walked towards us and we held each other so tightly we could hardly breathe. I could hear Bobby in the distance explaining things to Devon, but we couldn't let go of one another. We were both sobbing, and Bobby came and hugged us both. She eventually told us she would have to go back to work, but would be home soon. Bobby told her we would all be there. We went back to his home and spent the afternoon exchanging stories. Bobby then made a call and after a few minutes gave the phone to me.

"Hi, Lillian. It's Thomas. How are you?"

I couldn't answer him. All this was too overwhelming for me. I cried so much I felt I must have used up all my tears. It took me a while before I could talk. I think Thomas must have thought I couldn't hear because he shouted into the phone. He said he would come soon to visit and told me he loved me. We talked some more when a car drove up outside.

Anna said, "He's home! Oh, what a wonderful day this is." She ran to the door and excitedly said, "You will never guess who is here!"

They entered the room, and I totally lost my composure. Devon was sitting close to me and asked, "Who is it?"

Bobby had to answer. I jumped up and my big brother, Joseph, grabbed me until again I could hardly breathe. When he finally put me down, I just stood there and shook my head. I told them that now I was sure I was dreaming because all this could not be true. We talked nonstop for what seemed like hours, and then Ruthie came home and we talked some more. Anna and Grandma had disappeared to get a meal ready, and then they called us all in to eat. I was overjoyed when Bobby thanked God for all his blessings before we ate. I found out that all my family were Christians and loved the Lord. When we told them we had just gotten married the previous weekend, they decided we needed to have a party. They wanted us to stay, but when we told them we actually did not live very far away, they decided we should come every evening for dinner. I looked at Devon, and he reminded me of how much we still had to do. We agreed that every other day would be workable and we appreciated the invitation. We went home that night exhausted. I was surprised by how tired I was when we had not really done any work.

Chapter 11

*W*E WOKE UP THE FOLLOWING MORNING AND FOUND the sun shining. We painted the little room for Bobby. I realized I had not told my brother about his namesake. He was in for a surprise. We decided to wait until we were all together again before telling the rest of the family about Bobby. I knew I would have to explain why I had a five year old. Mom gave me a package to be opened when we finished painting his room, so we opened it and found decals for the walls. He was going to be so happy here. He already loved Devon and Devon loved spending time with him. Once again we counted our blessings. I called Mom when we stopped for a rest and thanked her for the decals. When she asked how we had gotten on I couldn't get the words out fast enough. I was crying all over again, and Devon had to take the phone from me to tell Mom what happened the previous day. She was overjoyed and promised a big celebration when we could all be together and she could meet the rest of my family. I talked to Bobby and he seemed happy enough. He had to hand the phone back to Mom because he was playing a game with Steve. We worked until late and the room was done. I shampooed the carpet so it would be ready for the furniture the next day. We found a dresser in the garage, which I scrubbed and brought inside. Mom told us there was a bed in the attic, so we brought that down and cleaned it. It was so much fun, and I don't remember for one minute wishing we were on a beach somewhere. I was loving every minute of my honeymoon.

While we were eating, Devon said he was thinking of talking to the pastor about church membership, but now he wondered if I would want to go to that church or worship with the rest of my family. I told him this was Mom's church and they had been a good church family to both of us. I understood why he would ask that question and I told him I was torn in my decision. We decided to think on it some more. We went to Bible study and were exercised by the message Pastor brought. He reminded us that we are God's workmanship, created in Christ Jesus. We are his disciples and our duty is to tell the good news of the gospel to as many people as we can and to pray without ceasing. When he finished the lesson, he asked for personal testimonies of prayers answered. There were quite a few who spoke and told how God had answered prayers, sometimes almost instantly and others after years of praying.

Devon looked at me, then put his hand up. Pastor told him to go ahead. He said, "Ever since I met my wife in college, she and I have been praying for her to be able to find her little sister, who was separated from her when they were placed in different foster families. Yesterday morning we prayed for her again before we went shopping. We walked into this hardware store and found it was owned by her brother whom she had also lost track of. He took us to his home where we found that her brother had married her best friend from school, and that her grandmother, whom she had never met, lived there also. Before we left last night, my wife had been reunited with her sister and another brother, who had been lost for years. We are here to testify to the fact that not only does God answer prayers, he gives us more than we ask for. He is truly a loving father, giving more abundantly than we could ever ask or think."

There was such an elongated silence that Devon thought he had taken up too much time. He started to say he was sorry for taking so long, but was interrupted by the pastor, who said. "Folks, this is something we as a church and I personally have been praying for for many years." Several of the members said, "Amen." And the pastor started singing "Blessed Assurance, Jesus is Mine." Oh what a foretaste of glory divine. The pastor closed in prayer and soon we were surrounded. Everyone wanted to know all the details. It was wonderful being able to share with these wonderful people God's glorious provision. I think our dilemma was solved right then because on the way home, Devon said he would really like to be a part of that church. I agreed. And we decided to talk to the pastor the very next Sunday.

Next day was also sunny and warm, so we worked outside and, after a trip to the local nursery, we planted some flowers and made the yard look pretty. A guy from the church came by and asked if we still wanted him to cut the grass as he was pressed for time and would not be able to do it until the following week. Apparently he did this to help pay for college but he had done Mom's all these years for free. We told him that now we were back, we could do it ourselves. We thanked him for his love for Mom and for doing this for so long. We realized once again that there was no end to the blessings God gives to his people. We sat there on the porch and thanked him for his mercies which are new every morning.

There was a call from Anna, making sure we were coming for dinner at five. I assured her that we wouldn't miss it and would be there. She said she was so glad that God had finally brought us all together again. She was always a good friend, even though I remember not wanting to share her with Bobby, when all the time God was working out his purposes. The last few years had shown me that God has his plan and that his plan will come to fruition with our help or in spite of us. All we have to do is watch and pray and let God be our guide, and the blessings will be showered on us. We set out for Bobby's a little early because we wanted to buy the things we had left the day before. Bobby was there and had the things Devon chose the previous day in a sack. Devon found a few more things and brought them to the front. Bobby was there, grinning from ear to ear and Joseph, who also worked there, kept asking if Devon needed this tool or that. Devon told them he was not made of money and was happy with what he had. When he offered to pay for his purchases, Bobby refused and said, "You are family. You can have whatever you need."

Devon shook his head, saying, "Wow! I like your family!"

Dinner was unbelievable. Anna was a great cook, and I asked her to teach me some of her cooking skills. She permitted me to help her in the kitchen and, as Ruthie was helping too, we sent Anna to put her feet up for a while. When we were alone, I asked Ruthie how she was doing and if she had always been with Bobby. She told me she had not been in touch with anyone for a long time, but some girls from her high school had invited her to church and she decided to go with them. She said she was sitting there feeling uncomfortable because the leader had been talking about the love of God. She said she hated God and then the leader came and sat at the end of her row and she had to pass him to go to the restroom. It was Bobby. She said she knew that God had directed her to that church that night. I asked her if she had been happy with her foster family and she hesitated, said, "No!" and started for the family room.

Bobby told us his story about how the owner of the hardware store befriended him, allowed him to work there through high school, and then adopted him when no one else would. He started going to church with the Weldon family and the youth group were visiting a nursing home. He felt drawn to one of the women who lived there and later found she was his grandmother. To make the story shorter, he said she had sold some property and shared the proceeds with him. When Anna consented to marry him, they bought this house and his grandmother moved in with them. It was amazing. Grandmother wanted to sit close to me and when I took her hand in mine, she held it firmly the rest of the evening. When we reached home and sat down, Devon grinned and said, "I think we are going to be very happy here. I can't wait till Mom and Bobby are here too. I think your family is going to love them." I agreed and we discussed what kind of celebration we should have when everybody met each other. We drifted off to sleep that night full of ideas and blessings and thrilled with anticipation of things to come.

Next day we finished moving furniture and found that Mom's things fitted into my old room nicely. We moved her photos and pictures from the walls and washed all the bedclothes. We bought her a new comforter which fitted in with the wall color in that room. Everything was dusted and shiny and ready for her arrival. Then we started on our room. Devon wanted to paint it too and thought it might be easier for Mom if it looked different. We decided on a light green and managed to get it all done by dinnertime. We opened the windows to air it before bedtime but discovered there was still an odor from the paint. We looked at one another and decided that rather than mess up the bed we had made ready for Mom, we would sleep on the couches. I giggled as we lay down to sleep. I could hear Mom saying, "What are you like?"

Devon said "Good night" and asked me if I was all right with this arrangement for one night. He promised he would not do any more painting in the afternoons. We decided we would tell no one of our adventure, and we slept peacefully.

Next day the odor was gone and we put the furniture back in place. By noon all three bedrooms were ready and the kitchen was next on the list. Mom told us she had always wanted to move the refrigerator to another spot and if we wanted to do that we should. Devon thought that it would be better at the other end of the kitchen. He tried to move it but it was too heavy. He suggested asking Bobby if he had a dolly we could borrow. He also told me the kitchen walls needed painting but he would wait till the next morning. We had calls from both Anna and Bobby, making sure we were coming for dinner. Anna said we could come early if we wanted and could spare the time. We had finished for the day so we decided that we would in case we needed to go somewhere for the dolly.

When we arrived, Ruthanne, Anna's little girl, had just awoken from her nap and was hungry. We sat in the kitchen while she nibbled and questioned everyone in turn. She wanted to know if I was really her auntie. She was so sweet and I thought how wonderful it was that Bobby had his very own cousin. My brother Bobby arrived soon after and Devon asked him about the dolly. The two of them took off and, unbeknownst to me, moved the refrigerator to its new location in my kitchen. I had not realized they had been gone so long because Anna and my grandmother and I were deep in conversation, interrupted only by the sweetest angel, who was trying her best to understand why I had left the last day I had been to see her. She thought it would be much better if I just stayed with her. My grandmother told me how she met Bobby and how she had come to know the Lord because of him. She also told me the sad story of how my grandfather died and why she ended up in the nursing home. She was so full of joy even though she was unable to walk.

As soon as Bobby and Devon came back we had dinner, and then it was time for Ruthanne to go to bed. She went off with her mother to get bathed and ready for bed, only to reappear in front of me shyly asking if I would read a story from her new book. I was taken by the hand into the sweetest room I had ever seen. Ruthanne climbed into bed and sat there like a little princess while I read one story from her book and then another. She pleaded for more but I told her I would read another next time I came to visit. She was agreeable and lay down to sleep only after she had closed her eyes and thanked God for her new book and her new auntie. When I returned to the living-room a little misty-eyed, Bobby told me that Devon had told him about Mom, how she had adopted me and given me a home, and how we had moved to her niece's home so I could attend college. He asked me where I had met this woman. I told him my foster family did not want anything more to do with me when I was old enough for college and that she had befriended me in a doctor's office. I was glad he didn't pursue the reason I was there.

I told him she had given me a home and a church family and had shown me my need of a savior. She helped me all through college, and we were moving back to her home because I had been offered a job at the Christian school there. Bobby then asked where Mrs. Alford was going to live and I told him we would all live together. He nodded his head but I could tell he was deep in thought. It was a wonderful evening.

It was so hard to keep the fact that I had a son to myself. I wasn't sure how that would be accepted but I thought if they met him first, it would be easier. Devon and I agreed to come back in a couple more days and we left to drive home. When we arrived home, I found that the kitchen was rearranged and everything was in place. Devon told me that Bobby had insisted on helping and that he had made a few suggestions about extending the area so we could have more space for a dining area in the kitchen. Devon seemed enthusiastic about his ideas but knew we couldn't do the work right away because of the cost and without Mom's permission. It was something worth thinking about and when I called Mom the following morning, I mentioned the idea to her. She thought it was a splendid idea and would help with the cost. I told her that was not necessary, that we would wait for a while until we had the money to pay for it. Bobby was so excited because he was going to the zoo. It was a little petting zoo and he was going to see goats and birds. I told him I would love to be going too but had more work to do. He said, "I understand" in a very grown-up way. I just wanted to hug him. I asked Mom if she was coping all right and said I thought we would be ready in another day or two. I offered to go back and help them pack, but she said that everything was working out great and Bobby was having a wonderful time with her niece's children. They had taken on the responsibility of entertaining Bobby with gusto and were enjoying their new tasks very well. She wondered if they could stay another week before coming home and said that she would let me know if Bobby showed any sign of a problem. I relaxed a little after that and when I told Devon he was relieved also.

On Sunday morning Devon surprised me with breakfast in bed. He said it was the least he could do on our honeymoon. I was delighted and he climbed back in and we lay and talked until it was time for church. Pastor brought a message from Psalm 23. He said it was obvious that David had a personal relationship with God. "The Lord is my Shepherd" speaks of love and devotion. A good shepherd cares for his sheep, and looks out for them when they are in danger or when they are sick. David experienced this when as a young man, he was given the courage by his shepherd God to fight the biggest, toughest soldier in the enemy's ranks. David had no armor and no sword; all he had was his slingshot, which he used when to scare wild animals away from the sheep he cared for. With God's help, he felled that giant. David trusted God for his safety then, and trusted him when he was in hiding. David knew he would never be in want of anything when he had the Lord as his companion. Pastor reminded us that God created the world, put the stars in place, and gave us the sun and the moon. He also created man from the dust of the earth and woman from the rib of the man so the two could procreate and populate the earth. God created all of these by Jesus Christ. Satan blinded mankind and tried to circumvent God's plan, but God took care of this delusion by sending his son to be born of a woman, his creation, and to live and die so that the guilt of those deluded by Satan could be cleansed by the blood of this perfect, sinless lamb of God. Pastor went on to quote Hebrews 13:6 ("The Lord is my helper. I will not fear what man can do unto me"), John 10:14 ("I am the good shepherd and know my sheep, and am known of mine."), and John 10:11 ("I am the Good shepherd, the good shepherd giveth his life for the sheep"). David knew about shepherding, but he also knew this good shepherd and followed him as in verse 7: "My sheep follow me for they know my voice."

Pastor underlined the personal touch in the words of this Psalm and followed that through with other scriptures. In 2 Corinthians 6:8, we read that God will be a father unto us. Pastor said God has been the source of help, support, and sustenance for many thousands of people over the centuries, and will continue to love and care for his people till the end of the world. In the Psalm, David tells us that God gives him rest from his labors and stills his troubled soul with the sound of still waters. We know how the waves of anxiety can be stilled by running water and the sounds of nature. God made all of these comforts for his people. David knows the truth of

God's word. He has experienced God's leading in his life. He trusts God with everything he has, even his life. He states in the Psalm, "Yea, though I walk through the valley of the shadow of death, I will fear no evil, for thou art with me." David knows the benefit of a rod and staff because he trekked across the hills shepherding his father's sheep in his younger days, but at present God's reliable rod and staff are all he needs. Pastor then took us to 2 Timothy 1:12: "I know whom I have believed and am persuaded that He is able to keep that which I have committed unto Him against that day." Pastor encouraged us with the fact that God is able and that if we are his, he will keep us. God is not only our creator, but he is our shepherd. He is our personal shepherd and our present and future are safe in his loving arms. We have a final resting place in his hands for he told us in John 14, "Let not your heart be troubled, I go to prepare a place for you and if I go I will come again and receive you unto myself." What thrilling words are these. Then he asked us to pray with him.

I had not taken my eyes off the pastor except to look up the scriptures, but after the prayer was over I looked at Devon and his eyes glistened with tears of emotion. I squeezed his hand. We had experienced in the last few days so many of God's blessings and examples of his watching care over us that we could not help but be emotional. We sang a hymn by C. D. Martin.:

Be not dismayed what e'er betide,
God will take care of you!
Beneath His wings of love abide
God will take care of you!
All you may need He will provide,
God will take care of you!
Trust Him and you will be satisfied,
God will take care of you!
Lonely and sad, from friends apart,
God will take care of you!
He will give peace to your aching heart,
God will take care of you!
No matter what may be the test,
God will take care of you!
Lean weary one upon his breast,

God will take care of you!
God will take care of you,
Through every day, along the way,
He will take care of you;
God will take care of you!

Pastor dismissed us after reading the words of this hymn by A. J. Flint:

God has not promised skies always blue,
Flower-strewn pathways all our lives through;
God has not promised sun without rain,
Joy without sorrow, peace without pain.
But God has promised strength for today,
Rest from our labors, light for our way,
Grace for our trials, help from above,
Unfailing kindness, undying love.

My heart was full as we left that day, and as we said goodbye to our church family we realized we were not the only ones whose hearts had been touched. Everyone seemed reserved and quiet. We made arrangements to visit with Pastor about church membership on Thursday morning and spent the rest of the day talking about the things in our lives which were unmistakably God's interventions. We read more of his word and decided that reading our Bibles every day, together if possible, would have to be one of our priorities. When I talked to Mom and told her of the wonderful sermon and of our decision to join with this particular group she was overjoyed. Bobby, she said, was starting to ask where his Mom was more often. She wondered if we would be ready soon, and said she didn't care if her room was ready or not. I told her I would talk to Devon and call her back the next day. She said they would be busy for the next couple of days because they had made plans to go to the park by the lake and stay overnight. She thought that by next weekend, Bobby would be ready to be back with his momma.

Next morning we tidied the garage and the workshop at the back. Devon was surprised at how many tools there were. He moved things around but felt he needed to talk to Mom about this space because it had obviously belonged to her late husband. I agreed and we decided we would take the afternoon off and go for a picnic in the park. It was sunny and warm and we had a relaxing time. We came home around four and found there was a message from my brother Bobby. He wanted to come see us and talk something over. We told him to come that evening and we had an early dinner so we would be ready when he came.

Bobby arrived shortly after six and seemed really excited about something. We were intrigued and wondered what this surprise was going to be. All my family were accounted for, so there could not be more surprises. He said he wanted to do something for us and he had a great idea, if we would allow him to carry it out. We both said "What?" at the same time and we all laughed. He said he wanted to do the extension for us and he could start the following day. He had the bricklayer, electrician, and plasterer all lined up and it could be finished in three to four days. We looked at one another and thought on the sermon we had just heard the day before and couldn't find the words to speak. Bobby was a little taken aback and started to apologize but Devon told him it would be wonderful and we were a little emotional about the goodness of God. Bobby told us he understood, and then told us that the money for this endeavor had actually come from our grandmother. Her money had bought his spacious home and paid for the hardware store franchise. He said it was God's money and wanted to know if he could go ahead. We called Mom and she agreed so we told him to go ahead. He and Devon did some measuring and moving stuff. He needed a few of the cabinets emptied, and I stayed busy all evening doing just that. He even brought boxes to store the things in and he carried those in from his truck. He left telling us that he would be back at eight o'clock in the morning, ready to start, and if I wanted to cover the furniture and counters with sheets that would be a big help. We went to bed that night feeling like we were looking at someone else's life instead of living it. Devon said, "I have never realized before just how much God is involved in all the everyday things of life. I mean he has brought you together with your whole family and with your grandmother. He has provided everything we need almost without us doing anything: this home, all the stuff both churches have given us, and now this. It is almost more than I can take in."

I agreed and reminded him of my favorite promise of scripture in Ephesians 3:20: "He is able to do exceeding abundantly above all that we ask or think." God is definitely our good shepherd and we made a pact that night to serve him to the best of our ability, in work and in church and everything else we are involved in.

I called Mom the next morning and caught her just before they left on their trip. She was glad I had called because she wondered if it would be all right for them to stay at the lake until the weekend. I told her I thought that was a wonderful idea and I was calling to see if she could hold Bobby off for another day or two till the work was done. She laughed too and said God was already taking care of everything. She told me not to worry about Bobby. He was in the best of spirits and would have a wonderful time. When I told Devon he grinned and threw his hands out, saying "What can I say? God has this."

Bobby arrived with Joseph and two other guys and an ice chest full of food, which Anna had prepared. I was amazed and asked what I needed to do. I was told nothing would be required of me. I decided I would stay out of the way while all this work was going on. I decided to go look at the school and see what the layout would be. I didn't think many would be there but there were a couple of cars and I decided to go in and look around. I introduced myself and was welcomed with open arms. I spent the morning there and was able to get a list of the students I was to teach. Someone had donated supplies for each teacher and I was able to organize everything and felt I had accomplished a lot that morning. I went home to check on the boys and found them hard at work. They had already framed the extension and had arranged for an inspector to be there first thing in the morning. That was a miracle in itself. Bobby told me that Anna had called and wanted me to call her. When I did she invited me to go shopping and have lunch with her. I was happy to oblige and met her at the mall. We enjoyed the afternoon together, reminiscing about school and our friendship. We also talked about that awful day when we left her home to go get my Mom and found her dead. I had not thought about how that had impacted her family. She told me it was some time before they knew what had happened, but her parents had never ceased to pray for me and were so excited to hear we were all reunited. I went home to see what was going on around six and was truly amazed at the progress those men had made. It added so much space to the kitchen area and left more room in the living area. We had dinner from the ice chest and they continued working until nine. The electric was in, the roof was done, and the drywall was up, and they were all still smiling. Bobby said he would be unable to be back until ten o'clock next morning because he had to talk to some representatives at the store but the electrician would be there at seven a.m. to talk to the inspector who was scheduled to be there shortly thereafter. Devon was tired but very happy and told me he liked my brother very much and had learned a lot from him about maintaining our home and various other things. He now felt capable of fixing things when they broke. He confessed that this had been a worry to him as we started our life together. We thought about how our life had changed in the last few weeks, and thanked God for his blessings which truly were new every morning. We retired early and set the alarm for six a.m. so we would be ready for the early workers.

Next day I rummaged in the workshop again and found a little bookshelf which I might be able to use at school. I cleaned it and set to work making name cards for my students. My desk was against the wall so the bookshelf would sit right at the end and hold all my supplies. There were cubes along one wall and the name cards would go on them. I was really looking forward to the first day of school. I did some timetables and some extracurricular fun projects to help make classes more enjoyable. By the time Bobby arrived the inspections were done and everything was in order. He sent the others home and he and Devon proceeded to add the trim and paint the walls. They were done by lunchtime. Bobby told us to use the rest of the food and keep the ice chest for use later. Then he gave us both a hug and left. We looked at each other after he was gone and shook our heads. It had been a whirlwind project and it looked wonderful. I knew Mom would be pleased. She called with an update on the fun that was being enjoyed by all and said the final arrangements were made for them to arrive home that afternoon. She said her niece wanted to come as well for a short visit before going on to her mother's. They were scheduled to arrive home on Thursday afternoon and Sharen and Steve were taking us all out for supper before motoring on to her mother's.

That night at church we were able to tell our friends about God's wonderful provision, and we were encouraged by Pastor's message which reminded us that God had his plan made before he even created the world. He showed us with many examples how God is involved in the minutest details. He told us about a spider which makes its nest in the ground and makes a trapdoor which it pulls down when it enters the nest. God made that spider and even though there are many people who don't like spiders, it is amazing that God gave the spider the ability to protect itself. He told us about the chameleon which has the ability to change colors so it can hide from predators. He reminded us that we are so much more precious to him than these so we need to trust him in every aspect of our lives. He gave us a verse in Matthew 10:30 which tells us that the very hairs on our heads are numbered. We lose hairs from our head every day and don't think of them at all, yet God counts them. He concluded with the words of a children's hymn:

> Our God is an awesome God
> He put the stars in place
> Our God is an awesome God
> He made people of every race
> Our God is an awesome God
> He hears our penitent prayer
> Our God is an awesome God
> He stays with us everywhere.

His words rang true in my heart. I felt that he has guided me every step of my life. I don't know what I would have been or where I would be had it not for his Holy Spirit guiding me. Again the congregation was quiet and thoughtful after the closing prayer, no doubt realizing the marks of God in their own lives. As we left, Pastor reminded us that we were to see him the next morning. On the way home, Devon told me that one day when he was about ten or eleven years-old, he was swimming in the river and got tangled in some weeds. The current was strong and he was dragged under. He had managed to get his head above water a few times. He said he was very scared. He remembered his mother telling him to always swim with a friend and he had disobeyed. He didn't remember passing out but the next thing he knew he was on the bank, a dog was licking his face, and a man was telling him to breathe. He remembered being exhausted and the man had carried him home. He hadn't thought about the incident for a long time but it had come back to his mind during the preaching. He realized God had been there with him that day and had sent an angel, a human one with a dog, to save him. As soon as we stopped the car he bowed his head and thanked God for what he had done for him that day and for intervening in his life. I was trembling as I remembered what I was considering that day when I was contemplating killing my baby, and so glad that God sent his angel, Mom, to save Bobby. He truly is a wonderful God and cares greatly for his children. We talked briefly to the Pastor the next morning and after asking us each some questions, he outlined what would happen the following Sunday morning. He was pretty sure there would be a meal provided and he was delighted to hear that his long lost church member would be back then too. It was all finally coming together and my boy was coming home. I had missed him a lot even though the honeymoon had been filled with so many surprises. We ate our lunch and then sat on the porch to wait. Devon said he was glad we were finally all going to be together, and hoped that Mom and Bobby would like their rooms. At last they pulled up and Bobby almost fell out of the car in his haste to reach us. There were hugs all around and then he asked Devon if he was able to stay. We all laughed but then realized we had not explained that part of the wedding to him. Devon grinned and told him that he was actually going to be living here. Bobby replied with an excited "Cool" and did some exploring inside the house. Mom was thrilled with her room. Bobby found his room and asked, "Can this be my room?" We were so happy. Mom loved the new extension and the extra room it provided. Sharen and Steve were impressed with how quickly it had all been done. Bobby buzzed around as if he was a bee going from flower to flower. He was so excited and every time he came near me I got another hug. He showed Sharen's kids his room and they helped carry his bags in; he seemed to have more than Mom.

Before long it was time to eat and Steve asked us where we could eat. Mom thought we should go to the café and everybody agreed. The owner was glad to see Mom again and cooked a wonderful meal for us. Sharen and Mom wanted to know more about my family and Steve and Devon chatted away about garden stuff and tools. Bobby talked away to his friends and all of a sudden looked really tired. Mom said he had been up since six that morning, as had all the kids. Sharen figured it was time to get on their way and we said our goodbyes and waved them off. It didn't take long for Bobby to shower and get to bed. He pleased me tremendously when he was praying by thanking God for his wonderful life and his wonderful mother and grandmother and new dad. He fell asleep quickly and I left him and told the others what he had prayed. Mom told Devon that Bobby really loved him and had asked many times when he would be able to see him again. I had a happy husband that night. It was wonderful. Life was wonderful. We were all together and we still had a few weeks to get routines in place before we started work. Devon's first day was the beginning of September and mine was halfway through August.

Anna called the following morning and asked us for dinner on Saturday. I told her there would be two extra people and she was thrilled. She asked if both were adults and I felt as if I was deceiving her by not telling her that I had a son. I said, "No. One of them is my son Bobby. He's six" I expected her to say something negative but instead she said that would be wonderful company for Ruthanne. She said we would be eating at six but she would love us to come early so we could visit. I said we would. I hung up the phone thinking that telling her about Bobby was easier than I thought it would be.

Friday went very smoothly. Mom indicated she would like to cook dinner sometimes, and suggested I make a family timetable. We worked on that, and figured out when we would do our grocery shopping. We made a washing schedule, a cleaning schedule, and a shopping schedule, and changed it several times. I just loved her. She was so accommodating and told me she loved lists and we would probably change them many times as we went along. She was so happy to be staying with us, and I was so happy she had agreed to stay.

Chapter 12

*W*E ARRIVED AT MY BROTHER'S HOME AT FOUR o'clock on Saturday and we were all welcomed with open arms. When Mom and my grandmother met, they were so happy. They had been neighbors a long time ago and lost touch when tragedy hit both of them. They spent the day reminiscing about old times, when they and their husbands would get together. It was so much fun to see them so happy. Bobby and Ruthanne hit it off within minutes and played happily together all day. There was not one raised eyebrow or questioning look regarding him. I had been so worried and for no reason. Life was so good. God had truly blessed me and as I watched Devon and my brother together I knew they had found a buddy in each other. When we drove home, Mom could not stop talking about how wonderful it was to have reconnected with her old friend. I told her it was pretty miraculous and she agreed.

"I used to help her when her son was unruly and she didn't know how to handle him. Her husband was such a quiet, gentle man and their son was wild sometimes," she said.

All of a sudden she realized she was talking about my dad and was so embarrassed. I told her she was right: he was wild and unhappy and I was finding it easier to pray for him. I wondered if he was alive, or if he had changed, and silently asked God to forgive him and save him, so that he could end his days as happy as I was just then.

The next few weeks went very fast. Devon started work a couple of days before me, for orientation, and Mom and I went over our schedule again.

She was happy to be back with her church family and had been invited to visit with a few of her friends. I was glad of that because she was going to be alone for most of the day. That had not been the case for a long time. She seemed excited to have free time and I realized how much of her life she had given up for me. I said as much and she told me her life had been so wonderful over the last five years, that God had filled her life with joy, and she didn't feel she had given up anything. She was such a sweet and selfless soul. I loved her as much as I'd loved my own mother.

School started in an earnest and it was not difficult at all having Bobby in my class. He was quite proud of the fact that his teacher was his mom. I loved those kids. Every day was filled with their joy of learning. Bobby tried so hard to please me that sometimes I thought it must stress him out a little. I didn't verbalize my thought but one day just before Thanksgiving, we were working together in the kitchen and Mom told me Bobby had told her that afternoon that he had the best teacher in the whole school. She asked him why he thought that and he said I loved all the kids but he got to come home with me so he got that love longer than anyone else. She said she was glad I was able to be his teacher for this year because it had made him so happy. That conversation put all my fears to rest and I had no worries after that.

Thanksgiving came and we spent the day with Bobby and Anna. I asked Mom if she was happy with that because I thought she might want to be with Grace and Sharen. She told me I was her family and she was glad to spend it with me. She was so animated when she got together with my grandmother, and they talked nonstop about everything under the sun. It was so easy to settle into the routine of family life when people were so incredibly happy.

I woke up the first day back at school feeling a little lightheaded. I jumped up as I usually did and was overcome with a wave of nausea. I was so disappointed: being sick with the flu was not in my timetable. I sat down on the side of the bed until the nausea passed. I asked Devon to wake Bobby and he left the room. I stood up again and had to run to the bathroom. Devon came back and immediately told Mom. She stepped in, made breakfast, and got Bobby ready for school. She told me to rest and she would call the school to let them know. She said she would also take Bobby to school. I felt better thirty minutes later but as soon as I stood up, I had to run to the bathroom again. Mom came home and brought me something to drink and told me that they had found someone to stand in for me for a couple of days. I relaxed a little but was really disappointed because the kids were practicing for the Christmas concert and I felt bad that I was letting them down. I kept trying to get up but the nausea always won. I lay there sipping the peppermint tea Mom had made for me. I went back to sleep eventually and woke up around eleven. I slipped out of bed and had no nausea, so I decided to shower and dress. I found Mom sitting at the table, reading her Bible. She asked me if I was feeling better and I told her that I felt like a fraud because I did not feel ill at all. Just then Devon called to see how I was doing. I told him that I felt fine and he was so relieved. I hadn't realized how worried he was. Mom asked me if I'd like something to eat and I told her I was starving. I hadn't had any breakfast so I was really hungry. She made us sandwiches, which I devoured. She was smiling to herself when she carried in some pudding for me.

As I ate it I looked at her, waiting for her to tell me what she was smiling about. She had brought another sandwich for herself and I realized I had eaten hers as well. I asked her, "What is wrong with me? I feel like I could eat a horse."

She asked me if I'd had a period lately. I thought about it and realized I couldn't remember when my period was. I had been so engrossed in school and everything else that I had just forgotten. Then she said, "Do you think you might be pregnant?"

I was struck dumb. There were so many emotions happening in me right then, I didn't know what to say. Mom gave me a hug and went into the kitchen. I heard the door close gently and the car leave. I figured she had somewhere to go, so I tried to figure out when my last period was. I realized I had missed two months and could hardly contain my joy at the thought. I washed the dishes and had just sat down again when Mom came back and presented me with a package. It was a pregnancy test. We both laughed and I went to the bathroom and did the test. It was positive. I couldn't wait to tell Devon and Bobby. Bobby was going to have a little brother or sister. He would be so happy. My next words were "Mom, will you teach me how to crochet?" I wasn't sure where that thought came from. Mom said it was just my mind racing to prepare for a new baby. Mom was laughing as she left to pick Bobby up from school and said that she had promised him they would go to the park on the way home. They arrived at the same time as Devon. I was jumping up and down as they met in the driveway and stopped to talk. Mom was trying to move them indoors and fairly pushed Devon in the door. He was looking at me with a puzzled look on his face and then Bobby ran over and hugged me and asked if I was feeling better. I told him I was more than better, that I was having a baby.

Devon just stood there stunned. Bobby had a weird look and then he asked, "Do I have to leave then, if you're getting a new baby?"

That brought Devon to his senses and he grabbed Bobby and hugged him and hugged me, and said, "We are getting a new brother or sister, not just Mom."

"Can we choose? I like girls."

Devon told him God would decide and that we wouldn't know for a while. He swung me around and then said he was sorry, that he shouldn't do that. He was laughing and crying and when Mom came back in, she had been doing the same in the kitchen. Bobby wanted to know if the baby could play with him, then he went to his room for toys. Devon asked if he should call his folks. He was so excited and so was Bobby. We told Bobby it would be a long time before we would need the toys but he should keep them safe in his room. He prayed that night that his baby would come soon. Mom had bought some ginger cookies and ginger ale and told me to set them by my bed for the morning. She told me to take them before venturing up out of bed. I said I would try to go to school next day but Mom said they had replaced me for two days and I was to call the next day if I needed more time. It was so wonderful to have her there. I didn't know anyone could be as happy as I was that evening and Devon's grin had never been so wide. Next day I lay in bed for a little while before getting up. I sipped my ginger ale and nibbled on my cookies. After about thirty minutes, Bobby came in rather worried so I got up and talked to him. I told him I was not ill and he accepted that and went to eat breakfast. He came back to tell me he was leaving for school and he would tell the other children I would be back soon because I was not ill, just tired.

Chapter 13

I<small>T WAS</small> C<small>HRISTMAS</small> E<small>VE AND</small> G<small>RACE AND</small> S<small>HAREN</small> had come by with gifts for Bobby and the baby. We had a lovely time and I appreciated so much that they came to visit. Bobby was so excited to see everyone again. He talked nonstop about his friends in school and his new baby and how they were going to play together. I could tell that all of Sharen's family loved him so much. They allowed him to have center stage, because they knew he was glad to see them. They made sure that Mom was happy to spend Christmas with Bobby and Anna. In fact they asked her several times. She told Grace that my grandmother was her old neighbor and that she really enjoyed spending time with her. When they left they were fully satisfied that she was happy with the arrangement and actually it made me feel better too.

Next day was busy from early morning. Mom and I had plans to cook and bake, before going to my brother's. I discovered that if I ate before starting my day, I was able to avoid the nausea. Mom's ginger sticks, which she had bought in a health food store, were a great boon. We decided to have breakfast first, then open gifts, and then cook. Devon was so funny; he walked backward and forward like a caged lion. He was more impatient than Bobby while we ate breakfast and prepared for opening gifts. Finally we were ready and Devon disappeared out the door. I was a little put out because he had been so impatient and I commented to Mom. She said nothing but continued pulling out the gifts from under the tree. I told Bobby he could start and just as he tore off the first strip off paper, Devon opened the door and struggled in with a bulky, half-wrapped huge thing. He hadn't taped the paper very well and it was flying loose all over the thing. He set it in front of me and said, "Merry Christmas."

I tore the loose paper off, thinking I had better teach him how to wrap, and what I found brought tears to my eyes. It was a beautiful cradle. It had rockers which was why the wrapping was so untidy. There were hearts along the sides. "Where did you find such a beautiful thing?" I said with a quivering voice.

"I made it," was his answer.

I was truly surprised. I couldn't believe he had been able to do all that in such a short time without me knowing. The rest of the morning was a flurry of flying paper, noisy toys, and cooking. Soon everything was ready and Bobby dragged himself away from his toys, begging to be able to bring just one with him. Mom carried the food to the car and Devon asked me if I was happy with my gift. He was like a little kid wanting to know if he had pleased me. I told him it was the most wonderful gift I'd ever received. I think I loved him even more after that.

The day was busy, and exciting. Ruthie had little time for Bobby because she had a new baby brother, who slept most of the time in spite of the noise. She found it difficult to leave his side, and it was quite a struggle to get her to come to the table for our meal. I think she thought he would disappear. Bobby peeked at the baby but did not seem very happy. I thought it was because Ruth Anne was not playing with him the way she usually did, so I took him off to a corner to ask him. He looked at me with such a sad face, and said, "So God gave our baby to Ruth Anne."

I have to admit I was speechless. Devon, who had obviously been watching closely, was at my side and asked was the problem was. I tried to get the words out but Bobby beat me to it, and told Devon that God had given our baby to Ruth Anne and we had no one to put in the new cradle which Devon had made. He was sorry after all the work Devon had done to get it ready. Devon started to laugh then realized the seriousness of the situation and quickly told Bobby that God had another baby for us, but we would have to wait a while. He said it would be much better to have a new baby when we were on summer vacation then we wouldn't have to leave him or her to go to school. That made perfect sense to Bobby and off he went to play, as happy as a bee. I told Devon I never knew what Bobby was going to come up with next. He agreed and said he was impressed by his concern about the cradle. He voiced my thoughts in that; one never knows what is processing in a child's mind. My grandmother and Mom had been missing for quite a while, and although at first I knew they were busy somewhere talking, I grew a little concerned when two hours had passed without seeing them. I asked Anna if they were all right and she said that Gran had a new project, which she was without a doubt showing Mom. I was intrigued but decide to wait and see.

The two ladies came in through the patio door, looking very pleased with themselves. They invited us to come see their Christmas present. We followed them thinking it was a hot tub or some other outdoor pleasure, but they walked down the path and behind the pool, where their pretty flower garden was, and there was a new building. We were ushered inside and it was the prettiest room with windows looking out on the flower garden. It was fully furnished, with pretty wallpaper on the walls. The kitchen was compact but had everything needed. There were two bedrooms, one furnished and the other bare. I asked if Gran was moving there and two voices said, "Yes." I looked at Mom and she was grinning like a Cheshire cat. My mind was racing. Did she not enjoy living with us? Had I offended her in some way? Gran wheeled herself toward me and told me she had invited Mom to live with her so the new baby could have her room. After the initial shock had worn off, I realized that these two wonderful women were disrupting their lives for us. I was so emotional, so overcome with conflicting thoughts that I was unable to speak. I had so depended on Mom these last few weeks, and wondered how I would manage without her. How selfish I was. She got along so well with her old friend and I shouldn't begrudge her that. She had helped me through a low period of my life and helped me make a wonderful life for Bobby. I felt sad and selfish and scared, but at the same time realized I had not even thought of a nursery for the baby. Mom was so thoughtful and unselfish and I knew I needed to be happy for her.

We went back in the house and Mom sat beside me and told me she would not leave until I was ready. She knew me so well. She said the room had been left for her to decide the furnishings and color scheme. She thought she would take her own furniture and leave room for the nursery furniture, but only when I thought the time was right. She said she could wait until the end of school, and then Devon and Bobby would be there to help. I hugged her. Even after all this time she was still putting me first. Gran was watching me intently, and I ran over and hugged her and thanked her. She told me she was so worried I would not approve and Mom would not come. She was looking forward to their new venture. They had obviously talked a lot about this. They had kept so quiet about the building and all the other details, I had to ask when they had started. They laughed and said they had talked about it many time since meeting but had decided to do something about it at Thanksgiving. I was amazed that they could build a dwelling so fast. We had much to discuss on the way home that night and in the days that followed. The cradle loomed large in the middle of the living room, underlining the fact that we were going to be a little overcrowded when all the baby stuff moved in. I thanked God for giving me Mom who had already taken care of the problem before it became a problem.

The weeks flew by, and although I was really tired I felt wonderful. By mutual consent, we decided Mom should move at Easter break. Bobby and Devon painted and wallpapered her room at Gran's and then we proceeded to turn her room into a nursery. Devon was learning a lot from Bobby and they had a lot of spiritual conversations together as they painted and pasted. Devon suggested I take a year off from teaching while the baby was little and needed all my time. He said Bobby had offered him a part-time job at the store evenings and Saturdays, as often as he wanted to work, so that would help with our finances which were in great shape because we had no mortgage. I thought long about it and knew that it would be good for Bobby, because he would gain independence with another teacher. I had the opportunity to spend a whole year with my baby. I could even learn to knit and crochet before Mom left. I asked her to teach me and she said she thought I'd never ask. She also told me that the following year, if I wanted to go back to school I could bring the baby to her every day. I asked her if she was sure and she told me it was her dearest wish. What a blessing God gave to me that day in the café when I was at a low point in my life. What a wonderful God we have; he has everything under control. He tells us not to worry, that he will take care of us, and we worry anyway. I asked God to help me depend on him more and not waste precious time being anxious. I was reminded of another promise from Philippians: "Be anxious for nothing but in all things, give thanks, for this is the will of God concerning you."

At my next doctor's visit, it was confirmed that my due date was June 30. I laughed when the doctor told me. She raised her eyebrows, questioning my laughter. I told her the date was another confirmation that God was in control of my life. I knew the school year was ending on June 23 so he had given me a week before the baby was due. Dr. Dodd, a Christian, agreed that all things work together for good to those who trust him. I was excited to tell everyone when the baby was coming.

Bobby as usual was the first to comment. He said, "How do they breathe with all that paper around?" I thought then that I should explain that God was actually growing the baby inside my tummy. His eyes opened wide when he heard that, but he didn't answer right away. I could tell he was processing that puzzling information. Devon asked if I needed to tell the school I needed coverage for the last month of school. I said I thought I would be all right, that I was confident God would take care of me. Bobby then interjected with, "So that's why you eat all the time, because the baby is eating your food." Devon and I exchanged glances, stifled our giggles, and agreed that I was eating for two. Bobby seemed relieved and I realized he had been aware that I was always hungry. He was always so aware of what other people were doing and wondering why they were doing it. He then asked if we could have Grandma back when the baby came or if there would still not be enough food for her.

Devon spoke first. "We have enough food for Grandma. What made you think that there wasn't enough food?"

Bobby explained that one day he heard me tell another teacher that I wanted to eat all the food in the house. Then Grandma said that she was leaving to go live with my other Grandma, so he thought it was because we didn't have enough food. Devon hugged him and said that what I meant was that I was always hungry because of the baby. There was always enough food. He also reassured Bobby that Grandma was going to be over a lot through the summer months and he could go visit any time. Bobby looked at me and saw that I was crying and hugged me, asking if I was sick again. I told him I was really well and happy and he shouldn't worry about things like that. Bobby said, "I was wondering when I could get a job so I could buy more food but if we really have enough, why is Grandma leaving?"

We spent the next half-hour reassuring him that we had enough food, that he didn't need a job, that his job was doing good in school, and that

Grandma wanted to give her room to the baby and spend some time with her old friend. He finally accepted that and that night he thanked God for giving us enough food. This incident reminded me to be careful what I say, and to speak clearly when I give information to others. When we told Mom about the incident, she was tearful and decided to talk with Bobby the following day to let him know how much she loved him.

The next few months were busy, but Mom kept everything running smoothly. Bobby would be in bed by seven and for the next couple of hours I would rest and watch Mom as she knitted soft blankets and clothes for the baby. I finally had the courage to try, and Mom showed me how to make slippers. My first pair were for Bobby. Mom showed me how to make them nonslip with acrylic paint, and he loved them. Next I knitted some tiny ones for the baby. Then I learned how to crochet and made a blanket. It was pink although I still did not know whether we had a boy or a girl. I thought this craft was difficult but, once I learned, it was so relaxing and I enjoyed creating things for my little one. Bobby had been invited to quite a few birthday celebrations with his school friends. He seemed to be popular among his classmates. There was one little boy in particular who invited him not with a card but with his own little scribbled note. Bobby wanted to give him his remote-controlled car because Micah told him he did not have one and, as Bobby had two, he felt like Micah should have one. I told him we could buy him a new one so Micah would be able to unwrap it on his birthday. He was pleased with that and asked if I would show him how to wrap it properly. We did this task together and on the day appointed we walked to Micah's home.

When we knocked on the door, Micah opened it and grinned so broadly. He told us to come in, and I placed the gift on the floor by the front door. I realized there was no party organized. Micah's mother came downstairs and was surprised to see us. Micah told her that Bobby had come for his birthday. She was embarrassed and I felt we were imposing on her, but Micah was so happy we were there. I prayed a silent prayer to ask God what he would have me do. I introduced myself to Micah's mom Angela and she said she was sorry but there was no party because she was a little short of money this month. She asked if we wouldn't mind staying for a little while for Micah's sake. I told her we would gladly stay. The boys played happily together and then settled down to a jigsaw puzzle which his Mom bought him for his birthday. He looked so happy. I realized there was not many extras in this home, and I encouraged Angela to tell me about herself. We found that we had much in common besides sons the same age. She seemed to become more comfortable as we talked, and I felt constrained to tell her my story. She cried and told me she was a single mother who had also been told to have an abortion but couldn't because she had learned all her life it was wrong. She told me a sad story of how she was so ashamed that she ran away from home and stopped going to church. She had worked two jobs, had her baby on her own, and was still struggling. My heart was burdened for her and asked her if she would like to come to church with us. She said she would love that.

By that time I realized there was no cake and that the jigsaw, which was being enjoyed so much, was the only gift. I told Angela I had an errand to run but I would be back very soon if I could leave Bobby there. She was happy that Bobby was staying, so I quickly went to the grocery store and bought a cake, candles, matches (just in case), and some Superman plates, cups, and napkins. At the checkout I added some soda and ice cream and went back to Angela's. I have never seen anyone so grateful for those few items. We both cried as we laid out the fare on the table. The boys paid little attention to what we were doing until Micah suddenly looked up and saw the cake and candles and whooped with joy, saying, "This is like a real birthday, like the one I went to a while ago. This is super, Mom, thank you! I love you!"

Angela started to say she hadn't provided the treats but I stopped her. Micah hugged his Mom for the longest time and I was convinced of how much I took for granted in life. We had cake and ice cream and Micah blew out his candles, but when asked if he had wished for anything, he said that all his wishes had come true so he didn't need to. That pierced my heart. Bobby suddenly remembered the gift he brought and ran to get it. Micah had that wrapping off in seconds and stood in awe when he saw what it was. Bobby showed him how to use the remote control and they played happily for the next two hours. I asked if we were keeping Angela from anything but she said she was happy for us to stay as long as we liked. She told me she could have been working that day but could not pay the person who looked after Micah and stayed home because it was his birthday. I told her Micah could come over and play with Bobby any time she had to work, so she wouldn't need a babysitter. I offered to pick her up for church and she told me she started work at 1:00 p.m. on Sunday, so I told her I could drop her off and Micah could come home with us. She cried and thanked me so many times. I told her I felt like God had directed Micah to write that invitation so we could meet. She hadn't known about the invitation until then but did admit that she had been praying that God would help her make him happy on his birthday.

As we walked home, I thought about how God had helped me and I resolved to do the same for this little family. Bobby confided to me that this was the best birthday party he had ever been to. What a blessing when God leads the way. That was the beginning of many wonderful days watching Bobby and Micah interact with each other in a very loving way.

Chapter 14

THE SCHOOL YEAR WAS FAST COMING TO AN END; I was getting to the stage where I waddled instead of walked and I was learning how to manage a household on my own. My friendship with Angela had grown. Mom would show up and stay for an hour at a time just knowing what things needed to be done. I loved her so much, and was grateful when she took Angela under her motherly wing. The last week of school arrived. Devon had to help me out of bed, and I thought about how glad I was that this was the last week before the summer break. I walked into the kitchen, holding my large tummy, breathing through the small contractions which had plagued me for a few days. I had barely sat down when I felt the oddest sensation. Another contraction happened and the floodgates opened. There was water everywhere. Devon had his back to me so I called to him. He spun around and looked horrified. That made me laugh and more fluid came out. I told him I needed to go to the hospital and asked him to call Mom. He was a nervous wreck and had to give me the phone because he didn't know what to say. Mom said she would be right over. Bobby thought I had peed on the floor and his eyes were open wide. I told him that the baby was coming. I remembered that one of the standby teachers had given me her number just in case she was needed. I managed to call her and then Devon called his to say he was not going to be in that day. Mom arrived and proceeded to put a plastic sheet and a blanket on the seat of the car. Devon helped me to wash and dress and then we drove to the hospital. Mom took Bobby to school so he could tell everyone that his baby was coming. She then followed me to the hospital and stayed with Devon while I labored.

Grace arrived at four o'clock and a little while after feeding her, I fell asleep exhausted. It was seven when the nurse woke me to feed Grace again and told me there were quite a few people waiting to see me. She would let them in two at a time. Bobby and Devon were first and Bobby was so loving to his little sister. Devon asked if he could hold her. He looked at her in wonder and tears ran down his face. He told me that my brothers and sister and Angela were waiting to see me but the nurse only allowed two at a time. He was going back out to let them in but he would be back. He kissed me gently as if he was afraid I would break. I loved him so much. Ruthie and Anna were next and they looked lovingly at Grace. Anna said they were not going to hold the baby yet, although they really wanted to. They left and Joseph and Angela came in. Angela gave me a pretty little white hat for Grace and I put it on her. Joseph just stood there speechless and I asked him if he wanted to kiss her. He said no very emphatically, then looked a little uncomfortable and said, "Oh, you mean the baby." It struck me as funny and I laughed.

Afterward when I was talking to Devon, we both thought that maybe we should try a little matchmaking. At the time, however, they made a hasty retreat and said others needed to come in. Bobby and Mom came in next and they also declined holding Grace because they had been instructed by Anna. They didn't stay long and Devon came back in with Bobby to say goodbye. I soon fell asleep with happy thoughts but an exhausted body.

My hospital stay was uneventful and I was soon home. I found that all I had the energy for was to feed myself and Grace. Mom came every day and Angela came for a little while on her two late-start days. On Friday I was able to summon enough energy to go to the school and show Grace to my class. They were thrilled and hugged me. I reluctantly said goodbye to them when we parted, knowing that wonderful year with them would now be history.

Joseph surprised me and came to visit. He stayed quite awhile; in fact, Mom had to shoo him away he stayed so late. He was reluctant to go. She wanted to know what was up with him, and I told her about when he and Angela had visited me and what he had said in my room at the hospital. She said that while they were waiting, they had been sitting together and had been involved in a serious conversation. She didn't know what the conversation was about, but thought it was interesting when she heard Joseph's remark. I told Devon I didn't think Angela and Joseph needed any help and he just smiled and nodded. Next time Angela came, Mom made sure we were alone for a while to see if Angela would say anything. She was right. Angela told me Joseph had told her about an experience he had had in the war and how God had helped him through that. She thought he was such a nice man. I asked her what had started that conversation because he didn't like to talk about that part of his life much. She said that when they found themselves sitting together, a little apart from the others, he was just trying to be friendly. He had asked her how she knew me. She had told him she was a single mother, struggling, and God just brought me along to help her. She said it was like God had sent an angel to help her. She told him her life was so happy now and that she had started going to church with me. She said he was so touched by what she had said that he had opened up about himself and what he had been through. She was impressed by his testimony and his quiet demeanor. I asked her if she would like to see him again. She said she would but that she didn't think he would be interested in her because she was, in her own eyes, tainted. I told her she should never feel like that and that if she was a child of God all her past was not only forgiven but washed away in the sea of forgetfulness. She was amazed to hear that and as we talked she told me she felt God was speaking to her heart and wanted to follow him. I believe that in that moment God enabled her to see she had salvation through the sacrifice of the Lord Jesus. She asked me why God would let his son be killed instead of us and I told her it was because he loved us. She left that day a new person in Christ. Afterward Mom, sensing my joy, inquired after Angela, and was overjoyed when I told her what had happened.

Grace was such an easy baby. She woke up, ate, and went back to sleep. Bobby and Micah spent their days together and were bosom pals. Devon worked at the store with Bobby and Joseph, and Mom came for a part of every day making sure we had food. Joseph came home with Bobby one day for dinner and they talked together for a long time. Devon's family came and stayed with Bobby and Anna, coming every day to see their grandbaby. They were so sweet and Mom came the first day with them and showed his mother where everything was in the kitchen, so she could feel at home and help me. I was so honored. His mother told me I had a gem of a mother. I told her that I knew that. God knew that I needed Lori Alford in my life. Devon was so proud to show off his little girl to his parents, telling them how to hold her and protect her head. His mom winked at me and just smiled sweetly.

I told Devon that Angela was coming the following Thursday for the afternoon because she had a half day off from work. Devon said he would make dinner that day and invite Joseph. He said that Joseph had asked him on occasion if Angela had been to see me. He knew Joseph wouldn't presume to ask if he could come but he thought he would be very happy to. When the day arrived Bobby, who knew what was happening, told Devon and Joseph they could leave early that day. Joseph couldn't come with Devon because he said he needed to go home for something. Devon chatted with Angela for a little while then started his meal prepping. I told Angela that Joseph was coming to dinner and she wanted to know if she needed to leave. She was visibly happy when I told her she was invited to dinner as well. Joseph arrived with two bouquets, one for me and one for Angela. He was so nervous I felt sorry for him. Angela chatted with him which seemed to put him at ease. We laughed a lot and discussed many things that evening, and when Bobby's bedtime came around Angela told Micah to get ready to go. Bobby asked in a pleading voice if Micah could spend the night. I looked at Angela, and she said it was all right if I didn't mind. Off they went to bed as happy as little bees. When Angela said she would wash the dishes, Devon said there was no need, but Joseph said he would help. Devon sat with me while they worked away in the kitchen. He was smiling quietly to himself as he stroked Grace's blanket. He said he remembered those days when he didn't know how to tell me how much he liked me. He said Joseph confided in him that he was feeling that way now. They came in quite a while later with cups of hot cocoa and cookies. They looked so happy. Joseph said they were going to leave so I could rest, and after a little while they did. About an hour later, Anna called to see how I was and to ask if I knew what had gotten into Joseph. He had come home and told Bobby he would be moving out and asked Bobby if he would help him find a nice home. I told her I thought the romance was moving very quickly.

Grace grew like a weed, reaching all her milestones and pleasing Dr. Dodd. I had regained my strength and was back to normal. I realized very quickly why Mom had encouraged me to take a year off. It was quite a feat to juggle feedings with all the other things. Devon helped quite a bit but I thought that when he went back to school, I would be busy. Angela didn't come as often, but when she did she was so joyful. Things had gotten quite serious with Joseph and he had started coming to our church to sit with her. That summer was gone in a flash and Devon and Bobby started school. Devon was able to drop Bobby off on his way to work. Mom picked Bobby and Micah up after school and usually, after asking permission of course, would take them to the little café for an ice cream. It was obvious they all loved one another and loved spending time together.

Life soon became routine until one day Angela came by and told me that Joseph had asked her to marry him. I was so happy for both of them. She asked me to be her matron of honor and wanted Bobby and Micah to be the ring bearers. Joseph asked Devon to be his best man. The wedding was to be in November. Anna, always the organizer, was asked to plan the wedding. Angela asked me to help her find a dress. She wanted to go to a thrift store and I agreed but later I thought of my dress just hanging there and wondered if she would like it. She was about the size I was before the baby. When she arrived ready to go shopping, I asked her if she would like to look at my wedding dress before she looked at the others. She looked at me surprised and said, "You would let me wear it?" I hugged her and went to the back of the closet and pulled it out. She tried it on and it fit perfectly. Then I retrieved the veil and headdress and offered those. She was shaking with excitement. Then I remembered the shoes. I said a quick prayer that they would also fit and they did. Angela was beside herself with excitement. She said she had been saving the money she used to spend on babysitting and I should have it all. I told her I didn't want any money and she should use it to buy the ring for Joseph. She squeezed me so tight I could hardly catch my breath. She said Joseph had a surprise for her that night and she couldn't wait to see it.

Angela called me at eight o'clock and asked me to guess what her surprise was. I didn't have a clue, so she told me Joseph had bought a house for them to live in. She wanted to know if I would come with her the following day to see it. I told her I would of course. I asked Devon if he knew anything about it and he told me he knew something was going on because he had been left in charge of the store on two occasions so Bobby and Joseph could go somewhere together. He was happy for Angela, and offered to help if they needed anything. Joseph wanted Angela to move in right away so she could organize everything the way she liked. He would stay with Bobby and Anna until after the wedding. I went the next day and really loved the house. It had three bedrooms and lots of windows and a swing and trampoline in the back yard. There was a barbeque pit at the edge of the patio and Angela thought it was a mansion. I was so happy for her. She said Joseph told her she could decorate it anyway she liked, but she loved everything about the place—except the curtains. They were ghastly green, so we measured the windows and took down the curtains in the back rooms of the house. There was so much light without the curtains that she was tempted to leave the windows bare. We talked about it and decided that sheers would be good. The walls were a pretty pale green, and would be a wonderful backdrop for furnishing their new home. I was so honored that Angela would allow me to help her do this.

When our friends in church heard about the engagement they went to work planning the reception. Joseph was puzzled when they told him. He couldn't understand why these people who he barely knew would go out of their way to provide such a thing. He talked about it every time I saw him. I think that is one of the reasons he decided to join our church instead of asking Angela to join his. Our pastor drew him aside one Sunday and on the way home, he told us he had been asked to tell his story to the church that night. He said he had done so before to the young people at his own church. He was nervous about speaking in church and said he felt inadequate because, when speaking to a church group, you are essentially God's ambassador to them. Devon told him God must think him adequate or he would not have prompted the pastor to ask him. He thought quietly about that for a while. After lunch we all made our now routine trip to Anna's, where we discussed the world's problems and watched the children. Joseph and Bobby disappeared and a few minutes and later called Devon to go with them. Later I discovered that they had gone to pray with Joseph. He was anxious to say the right thing later that evening.

Joseph was amazing. He held everyone's attention as he related how God had preserved him, how God had used him to help his captain, how God his heavenly Father had been with him through his long hospital stay, how in a miraculous way that only God can orchestrate, he had been directed to his missing family, and how God had now given him a wonderful Christian girl to be his wife. He gave thanks to God for all the blessings which had been showered on him and never once complained about anything negative in his life. I could tell that our pastor was emotional when he thanked Joseph, and instead of preaching, he read a passage of scripture and called on the congregation to pray for Joseph and his wife-to-be. It was a moving experience to hear those people cry out to God to bless them and protect them. The pastor concluded by saying that he believed God had a job for this young man to do and asked them to pray for him daily. Everyone left rather quietly, compared to the boisterous conversations which were the norm on a Sunday evening.

Joseph himself was quieter than usual when we reached home. After a cup of coffee, he and Angela decided to go. Angela wanted to know if I could keep Micah a little longer the following day, as she had back-to-back shifts with her two jobs. Joseph was surprised she had two jobs, and I was not surprised the following day when she told me Joseph had told her she could quit one of her jobs if she wanted to. She gave her notice and was so happy. She told me Joseph had told her that when they were married, she could quit both jobs and go back to school to do something she really loved. I was so proud of my big brother and so glad I had gotten to know him again.

It wasn't long until November and wedding preparations were in full swing. Plans were all completed. Outfits for the boys were obtained. Once Angela had met Ruthie and Ruthanne she included them in her wedding, asking Ruthie to be a bridesmaid and Ruthanne to be a flower girl. Angela told Anna and Ruthie that she had extra money and would help pay for their dresses, but Anna refused and said that it would be an honor to purchase the dresses for the girls. Our family was growing and I loved it. Mom was happy and Grandma was happy. When we visited, the kids wanted to spend time with the grandmas, and I suspect they had secret treats while there. Our babies were doing well, and I loved the fact that we were both breastfeeding and understood the need to do that at a moment's notice.

Chapter 15

THE WEDDING WAS A WONDERFUL TESTIMONY TO God's grace and favor. When Joseph said his vows, he included thanks to God for finding him a wife and asked the wedding guests to pray for guidance for them both. Angela did the same, thanking God for a godly husband and a father for Micah. Pastor brought a message on God's gifts to us, including the gift of his son, the Lord Jesus Christ, who in turn gave the gift of substituting himself in our place to atone for our sins and make us worthy to be called the children of God. Ruthanne and the boys did their jobs perfectly and were all smiles as they walked down the aisle. The friends at church provided a wonderful meal and Anna had made the most beautiful cake. When it was time for them to leave, Angela told Micah to come and stand by me, but as he was walking away she came after him and hugged me, whispering in my ear that she was glad Micah wrote that note to Bobby to invite him to his birthday. I told her that it was a God prompting, and that I was glad too.

Bobby and Anna had bought a combination bed and crib and we decided we would put it in the room which was to be the nursery and, because it was the bigger room, we moved Bobby's bed in there too. That way the boys could be together when Micah stayed. I was very tired when it was time for me to go to bed. Devon had already jumped in the shower when I carried Grace in. I guess I just put her in the bassinet and lay down and fell asleep. Grace woke me up for her feeding and I found myself laying on top of the covers fully dressed. Devon was asleep in the chair. I woke him and he brought a glass of milk and a cookie and then burped Grace while I undressed and washed my face. We both climbed into bed and he told me to switch off the alarm for the morning. We awoke the next morning to happy sounds of laughter from the two boys. Devon had the boys help him make waffles for breakfast and I fed Grace and showered while they were busy. I had time to dress Grace and myself before the three of them came looking for us.

Micah told me his clothes were in the blue bag and he couldn't find it. I was sure I had brought the bag in from the car, but it was nowhere to be found. Micah thought it was in the room where we opened the box with the bed in it, and Bobby said he had put Grace's bag and other things in the closet in his old room. Devon checked the nursery closet and there it was. Micah said Bobby was lucky because his dad was so smart and wished he had a dad. I told him he did, that Joseph was his dad now. His next question humbled me because he asked if that meant Joseph would live with them in their new home. I told him that Joseph couldn't wait to move in with them and be his dad. He was so excited and wanted to know if he would stay every day and forever. I assured him that it was a forever thing. He was so happy. Angela called later and he asked her if she knew that Joseph was going to live with them and that Joseph was going to be his dad. She told Joseph and he talked to Micah on the phone and made a little boy extremely happy.

We had a very happy carload going to church that morning, and when we got there Micah told everyone about his good news. They told him they were very excited to hear the news and a few of them gave him some instructions as to how to treat a father. God is so good and he had put it in the Pastor's heart to preach on the scripture which tells children to obey their parents. He went into great detail and spoke directly to the children, stopping and asking them questions during the sermon. There was no doubt left in Micah's mind when he brought the subject up on the way home. He asked Bobby what he would do if someone wanted him to do something which his dad did not allow. Bobby told him he would ask his dad if it was all right. Micah seemed satisfied with that, but Devon glanced at me with a questioning look and I resolved to let Angela know about the conversation so she could inquire further about what was on his mind. He didn't seem to be too worried as they spent the afternoon reading and working on a giant jigsaw puzzle, which Joseph had left for them.

After the evening service, Pastor asked Devon if he would be interested in helping with prison ministries. Devon wanted to know more about it so they arranged to meet for coffee to discuss it. He told me he had been wishing he could be more useful to God and serve him in some way, and that this might be something he could do. He wondered if he would be robbing me of our precious time together since he was working the extra job. I figured it would only be once a week so I didn't think it would be too time consuming.

Joseph and Angela came back on Thursday, earlier than expected, and said they would like to pick up the boys from school and take them home for supper. I called Mom and told her and she said she would go to the school to let the boys know what was happening and then would come for a visit. I loved her for being so thoughtful and being concerned that Bobby might not want to go because it was not the usual thing. She arrived with an ice cream treat for the two of us and loved on Grace while she was awake. She was concerned I had overdone things with the wedding and keeping the boys, telling me she enjoyed that time with them so much that she would miss them if she wasn't needed anymore. I told her not to worry, that I would always need her and that she could come any time to visit. She was glad when I showed her the room, and thought we had made a very good decision as that room was bigger. When we sat back down on the couch, she told me she was thrilled to be living with her old friend, and she was so glad we had brought so much happiness into her old house. She hugged me and said she was so thankful that God had brought me into the doctor's office at the same time as she was there. I thought back on that day and the misery and confusion I felt. Together we thanked God for bringing us his providence that day. What a wonderful heavenly Father we have. Mom had promised Grandma she would bring some groceries home, so she left about the time that Devon came home.

He was very quiet and pensive, and I wondered if there was something on his mind. We ate dinner mostly in silence and I asked him if there was something wrong. He said he didn't want to worry me but that he needed to make a decision about work. I knew he loved teaching and was sorry to hear he was unhappy about something. I persuaded him to tell me. He said the school had decided to change the curriculum and wanted to know if he would be willing to teach a History class in addition to his other classes. It would be an evening class three times a week and the other two evenings he would be teaching his own subject. He didn't want to turn down the extra classes because it would mean more money but didn't like the idea of never being home in the evening. I felt as if I was the cause of his distress because I was not working. He told me that was not it. He had looked at the books which the college had chosen for these classes and found they were very unpatriotic. In fact some of the history was unlike anything he had ever learned in school. He just wasn't sure if he wanted to be involved in teaching that subject. I could tell he was torn, and then there was the new ministry in which he may become involved. We prayed earnestly about that and other things like Mom and Bobby, and were still sitting at the table talking, when Angela and Joseph brought the boys. They stayed only fifteen minutes, but I noticed that Micah was following Joseph around like a shadow. Angela had noted it also, and told me she was so happy that they already loved each other so much. Devon and I decided he needed more time to consider and determined he would ask for time to think on it before making a decision.

On Monday Devon arrived home with a few of the books he was supposed to use for his Social Studies classes. We took turns reading them while Bobby worked on his jigsaw puzzle. Devon had me write down the pages and paragraphs which I didn't agree with. I seemed to be scribbling more than I was reading. Devon was engrossed in reading when I glanced at him. I told him there were a lot of things which did not seem right. He looked at my notes and read some of the paragraphs. He said my book was even worse than the one he was reading. "This is not American history, this is world history, but it is an American history class I'm supposed to be teaching. I don't think I can teach this stuff; I may have to decline the class. I was so hoping that the extra money would mean you could have another year off," he said. I told him not to worry about that and agreed it would be difficult to teach the history of the country without mentioning what part God had to play in the foundation of it. From what I had read, many of the founding fathers were Christians and sought to set up the governing body to please God. Devon agreed and suggested we pray about the whole situation. He said he couldn't teach it but that someone else would and he felt that that was wrong. He decided he would ask if he could speak at the next board meeting and see if he could change their minds about the curriculum. I was so proud of him, being ready to fight for what was right; he had always been so shy.

On Tuesday he had made arrangements to meet with Pastor at lunchtime and decided to discuss the subject with him. When he arrived home he was in a really great mood. He said he had been invited to speak at the board meeting and that the pastor was going to speak also. He also said he was going to help with the prison ministry and that the following Sunday afternoon he was going with a few of the men to a prison which was about an hour away. They usually left right after church and ate lunch in the car on the way. He wondered if he could bring a lunch with him to church and then go with them.

On Sunday morning I could tell he was nervous and when I asked the reason he said Pastor had asked him to say a few words about himself because he was there for the first time. He was worried that what he had decided to say was not what God would want. We prayed together and Bobby joined in and asked God to help his dad. That was all Devon needed. He looked at me and whispered, "He called me Dad." It was a very emotional moment, and I squeezed his hand as we climbed into the car.

"He has always loved you. You know that."

"Yes I know, but that's the first time I've heard him call me Dad."

Pastor greeted us as we walked in and asked Devon if he was ready. Devon nodded and we followed him in to the pew.

Pastor prayed for the prison ministry and for Devon in particular after the sermon, so when we were leaving, Angela and Joseph asked us if we would like to go home with them for lunch so the boys could be together. They wanted to know all about the prison ministry, and I really knew very little. Devon had told me that it had been going on for three years and there were always at least a half dozen men who came. They had one guy come to know the Lord during that time and that encouraged them to continue. We had a nice afternoon and stayed until we left for church. Grace kept Angela and I entertained and Joseph played outside for a while with the boys.

Devon was fairly bubbling with joy when we met. He said he was talking to the men about how God had saved him and worked out so many things in his life, and he felt constrained to tell them about the struggle he was having with the curriculum at school. Pastor encouraged the men to ask questions afterward and he said there was a lively discussion among the prisoners about patriotism. Afterward, he had used what they said about being patriotic to their country to illustrate how we should be more patriotic to God and his heaven, reminding them that their life on earth was for a short time and their life thereafter was forever. He told them the clear message of redemption through the blood of God's son Jesus Christ. Devon said they went from being very boisterous to being very subdued. He said he actually heard a sob while they were praying. When the prayer was finished, a prisoner who had been sitting over by himself and who had not joined in with the conversation that had taken place earlier left rather suddenly. Devon asked the pastor about him and was told he came every week and left every week before anyone could talk to him. He told me he felt led to pray for that man. So at breakfast and dinner and then in the evening when we did our daily Bible study, he diligently prayed for this man. Bobby thought Devon should try to find out his name so God would know who we were talking about. Devon said he would try to talk to him the next time they went.

Chapter 16

EVON AND THE PASTOR MET WITH THE BOARD AND they listened intently to what Devon had to say. He reminded them that the course he was to teach was American History. He said he had reviewed the textbooks which he was supposed to use and was disappointed in the fact that three whole chapters were dedicated to Islam and he had found only one paragraph mentioning the trials and discussions which related to the founding fathers of this country. The board were astonished and asked for copies of the textbooks in question. One member stated they were making a mountain out of a molehill and people ought to know about Islam because Muslims had done so much good for this country.

Pastor said, "Name one thing that they have done apart from the terrorist-like activities."

The board member was unable to think of anything. Devon asked to be excused and retrieved the textbooks and upon his return handed one to each board member. He pointed out the passages he had found which were not what he called the history of America, and before long a motion was made and seconded that these books would not be used in the college and they asked Devon if he would be in charge of finding a more suitable textbook. He was thrilled and received a "Well done" on the way home from Pastor.

Soon it was time for another visit to the prison. That morning at breakfast Devon was praying for the prisoner with no name. Bobby reminded Devon he needed to find out what his name was. I had made plans for Angela and Joseph to come for the afternoon, but Anna had called begging us all to come and celebrate Grandma's birthday with them. We were delighted and I wrapped the little gift I had made for her. It was a picture of Grace in the prettiest frame that I had spied in the market one day. Devon was told that he would be forgiven if he would come after church for a little while. He readily agreed.

Grandma was so surprised when she came in for her birthday lunch. She cried a little and said she was so blessed to have such a large family after thinking for years she had none. We had a lovely afternoon and then we all went our separate ways to church. Everyone was expected later in the evening. Grandma was so overjoyed that Anna had managed to get all her family to come at the same time to see her. She said this was the best birthday she had ever had. When we met, Devon he was unable to speak properly. He started to say something and I didn't understand him. He drew me aside and said, "You have got to hear this."

Bobby interrupted and asked him if he had found out the prisoner's name. Devon held my hands and said, "I think it was your father, the prisoner, I think it is your father." I heard him but couldn't comprehend the information. "I think you need to go see him!"

No! This wasn't happening. My father. My ears were ringing and I felt a little faint.

Devon shook my hands which he was still holding. "Lilly, do you hear me? I think I found your father! They have visiting hours and I asked him if I could visit with him. He said I could. You've got to come! Lilly, do you hear me?"

I was so stunned, I couldn't think. How could I see this man? What would I say to him?

Devon was looking at me, his face close to mine. "Lilly, are you all right?"

I asked him to hold the baby while I went to the restroom. What had happened to this beautiful day? How could I go see the man who killed my mother? Why was he in prison? Had he killed someone else? I was in so much turmoil. Betty, one of my church friends, came in and asked if I was feeling unwell. I told her my Dad had killed my mother when I was fifteen and the men had found him in the prison.

"You haven't seen him since you were fifteen," she asked.

"Devon wants me to go see him and I can't. He is an animal."

Betty put her arms around me and prayed for God's presence to be with me as I absorbed this news. Then she gently reminded me that we are all God's creatures and can all be forgiven by him if we repent and ask his forgiveness.

Chapter 17

I SAT THROUGH THE SERVICE, COMPLETELY NUMB.
Devon kept stealing glances at me and Bobby sat beside me and held
my hand. He didn't know what was wrong but he knew there was something
wrong. On the way out, Pastor took my hand and asked me if I would like
to wait behind for a few minutes so we could talk. I nodded, and he told me
to wait in his office. I sat down in there, still numb. I silently asked the Lord
to help me. I looked up at the wall and there in front of me was a canvas
with the Lord's Prayer. I read it through and quickly realized God was
speaking to me through it. He was reminding me that he had forgiven me
and in turn I was to forgive others. But he beat my poor mother. It was still
there on the wall. Forgive my sins as I forgive others. There was no escaping
this truth. I had been so blessed by God that I'd never even thought about
forgiving others.

Pastor came in with Devon. Grace was with Angela. Bobby was with
Micah. They were all worried about me.

"I am going to be all right. I just need time to think."

Devon said, "I am sorry for upsetting you. You were so excited about
finding the rest of your family that I thought...I'm such a fool. I just realized
that your Mom...I'm sorry Lilly. It's all right, you don't have to go. Please
forgive me."

I looked at him. He was in so much distress that I felt bad. "It's all
right Devon. God is just teaching me that one of the traits of a believer is
forgiveness, and I guess I need to forgive more than you."

He put his arms around me, right there in front of the pastor, and told me that he loved me more than anyone in the world, and would never deliberately do anything to hurt me. I told him he hadn't hurt me. He had just stunned me, and I needed time to assimilate the news.

"Are you ready to go? Everybody is waiting. I guess we are going to Bobby and Anna's."

I froze again. How could we go there with this kind of news? I told Devon that might not be a good thing. He said that he would not say a thing. Pastor, who had been sitting quietly, asked if he might pray with us. Devon encouraged him to do so. He prayed for me, he prayed for Devon and his new ministry, he prayed for the prisoners, and for Robert Swanson in particular. Devon held me tight when Pastor mentioned my father's name, but I was beginning to realize that if God had sent his son to die for sinners, then perhaps he died for my father. I felt extraordinarily calm about it now. Pastor finished his prayer, patted me on the shoulder, and left. He told Devon to pull the door shut when we left but to stay as long as we needed.

Devon asked me what I wanted to do. I said I would like to go to Anna's. He asked me if he should say anything about Robert Swanson to the family and to Grandma in particular. I felt that Grandma needed to know that her son was still alive. Devon told me my dad was a broken man. He had been attending the services for a year now and he believed God could not forgive him for what he had done. He told Devon he had ruined so many lives, including the lives of his parents and his children, and that he had caused his wife's death. He cries a lot, has no friends, and Pastor has been praying for him for months. Devon said that he had squeezed his arm and that he was shaking with emotion.

We all made the trip to Anna's and Devon allowed Bobby to go with Joseph and Angela. In the car we decided Devon should tell everybody when he had an opportunity, but he needed to be prepared for anything. I had not discussed my feelings about my dad with any of my siblings so I didn't really know what they thought of him. It was good to see Thomas again and when the children were busy, Devon stood up and said he had something to say. Everyone looked at him and then at me and then at each other, not knowing what to expect. He started by telling them that a month ago his pastor had invited him to help with their prison ministry. He told them about this man who felt unable to accept that God could love him. Then he said, "His name is Robert Swanson."

I felt the goosebumps again just like before in church. I think everyone felt them too.

Grandma was the first to recover. "You found my son?"

Devon replied, "I think I have."

Thomas put his head in his hands. Anna walked over to Bobby and put her arms around him. Joseph sat there in a daze and Angela looked on with a puzzled look on her face. Mom moved closer to me and put her hand over mine. Devon told them he had just found out his name that afternoon and hoped it wasn't too much of a shock.

Bobby was the first to speak. "I have hoped for years that this day would come. I struggled with forgiving my father for a long time, but I realized that until I could forgive him I would be holding back God's blessings for me." He asked how everybody else felt.

Thomas spoke next. He said he had ended up in jail at one point in his life and been released but was homeless with nowhere to go. He believed God had sent an angel in the form of his father-in-law to rescue him. "I hated my father but I also came to realize that God had forgiven me, and that all sin is the same in God's eyes, so I have forgiven him."

Ruthie was sobbing uncontrollably by this time and Anna went to her rescue. I went over to Grandma and asked her if she would come with me to see her son. She nodded and squeezed my hand. Then everybody started talking and we knew that we were all on the same wavelength. We all needed to go see this man and let him know that God could indeed forgive him if he was truly repentant. Before going home that evening, the schedule had been organized. Devon thought he could only have one visitor at a time but he would inquire and let us know.

Devon realized the next day that he couldn't wait another month to see Robert Swanson. He talked it over with the pastor, who had made the arrangements with the prison authorities to have the services. He didn't think there would be a problem as Devon had already been checked out by them so he could attend the meetings. He said Devon would have to call to find out when visiting time was and how many people could be there. By Tuesday he had already made the arrangements and found out he could have four visitors but only one at a time. That made me nervous because I would have preferred visiting him with Devon or one of my brothers at my side, but Devon reminded me that God was always at my side.

The following Saturday was the time appointed. Devon told Bobby and he told everyone else. They decided among themselves that Bobby, Joseph, and Thomas would go the first week with Devon, then the following week Ruthie, Grandma, and I would accompany Devon. I didn't know about the others but I felt excited and fearful all at the same time. In my mind, I went through many scenarios concerning that first visit with my Dad, and lost much sleep over it. We decided to set aside a time each day to pray specifically about the visit. I knew in my heart that God had been in this and that things would be all right but the memories kept flooding back. Devon reminded me one morning that these were probably the buffetings of Satan that the Bible talks about. Mom came over more often and we talked about Grace and all things baby. I knew she was trying to keep me from dwelling on the visit. She knew me so well.

Chapter 18

SATURDAY FINALLY CAME AND MY THREE BROTHERS came over to ride with Devon. They prayed together before leaving and I marveled at how God had answered my dear mother's prayers for her children. All of us now knew the Lord and that fact brought tears to my eyes. They were of course tears of joy. I gave each of them a hug before they left. About five minutes after they left, Pastor called to find out when they were going and told me several of the men from the church were meeting to pray for the visit. He asked me how I felt, and I told him I was a little nervous but felt it was the right thing to do. He told me I would feel better once the visit was over and I would be glad I had decided to go. He prayed with me before saying goodbye.

Mom arrived with Grandma and we had a wonderful visit. Grandma had never been to the house before and wanted to drive by her old home. Mom thought that it would be rude not to stop by. They were such a blessing. I saw how they loved one another and it was a joy to see how they interacted with one another. They stayed until Devon and the others came home. Each of them said he had a good visit, that Dad was very sorrowful, and that I shouldn't be worried about visiting with him. Grandma was visibly relieved, so I knew that she too was apprehensive about her visit.

When they all left, Devon told me my dad had thanked him over and over again for finding his family; this was his only wish left in this world because he knew he had to pay for his actions. Devon was so thrilled to have been used of God to do this. Devon told my dad that Lillian was his wife and

Dad cried like a baby. He told Devon he had listened to Pastor and the other men speak month after month and wanted to ask God for forgiveness but couldn't because he thought his sin was the worst and couldn't be forgiven. He was so emotional after my brothers' visit. Each told Dad he had forgiven him, that they loved the Lord, and that he could be forgiven too. Dad asked Devon to pray with him before he left. Devon prayed and then asked Dad if he wanted to pray. He declined saying God wouldn't hear his prayer because he had been so evil. Devon reminded him that God forgives those who are repentant. He prayed, Devon said, in a shaky voice and asked God to forgive all his past wrongs. He went on to say he would do anything make up for his actions. Devon went over the good news of the gospel with him and left, promising to let the pastor know he was grateful for his monthly visits.

The next Saturday, Devon drove us over to Anna's and my children were left in the care of Mom and Anna. Bobby and Devon switched cars and Grandma was helped into the front seat. Ruthie and I sat holding hands in the back. Again Devon went in first for a couple of minutes then I went in. When I sat down in front of him I realized I was holding my breath. I sighed and Dad said he was sorry for all the misery he had caused. He was so unlike his former self that all my fear was gone and I felt sorry for him. I told him I was a Christian and I forgave him for everything. He cried and was unable to speak for a few minutes. He said he believed God had forgiven him also. He said he had difficulty with that because he had hated God for so long, but now he felt peace for the first time in his life. I told him Ruthie was coming in next and he wanted to know how she was. I told him she would tell him herself and he should relax. I left and Ruthie was allowed to go in. Grandma was shaking but I think it was with excitement rather than fear. Ruthie came out smiling and Grandma wheeled herself in. Ruthie told me it was better than she imagined and they had held a conversation. He asked her what her life had been like and cried when she told him some of her history. He said it was all his fault but he was sorry. It wasn't long till Grandma came out. She apparently had not obeyed the rules of no contact and had been told repeatedly to refrain from touching the prisoner. She said she couldn't stop herself because she hadn't touched him in so many years; she needed to feel and know it was real. Devon went back in and Grandma told us she told Dad his dad died the day he left home. She said Dad sobbed when he heard that and she wheeled herself around to hug him. He cried all the harder, but the guard told her to sit on the other side of the table. He was unable to control his anguish and she went around again to comfort him. She told the guard she just told him his dad was dead. The guard was sympathetic but told her she needed to stay on her side of the table and if she moved again she would have to exit the room. She did it again anyway, stating she needed to hug her son and tell him that she forgave him, We were all very subdued and thoughtful on the way home and I knew part of that was because the visit was over and part of it was because of Dad's demeanor. There was no doubt he was a changed man. I thanked Devon when we reached home for being willing to go to prison ministries in the first place and then for taking an interest in Dad. Bobby asked for his name again and we both realized at the same time we needed to tell Bobby we had found his grandpa. He was so matter of fact about it and said he loved the idea that some of his grandparents were hiding but they were staying hidden for too long. He wanted to know when he could visit. Devon said it wasn't possible at that time but maybe one day we would be able to go. He accepted that without another question and went back to his jigsaw puzzle.

Devon told me he was going to accept the other position at the college, and told me that I didn't have to go back to work because of the extra money he would be making. I wasn't sure if I wanted to stay home, but did not make a decision right then. He went to the hardware store to talk to Bobby about his employment there. I sat down with Grace and Bobby and thought on my life. It was perfect. There were no longer any loose ends, darkness, or hidden cares. God in his mighty power had once again brought my family together. He is truly an all-fulfilling God who gives abundantly, certainly more than we could ever ask for or think. I silently asked him to help me to always show his love for me in every aspect of my life.

Epilogue

THIS ENCOUNTER WITH THEIR FATHER BROUGHT healing to all members of the family. God's power was exhibited in each family member. Grandma was happier than she had realized was possible. Bobby, knowing God had orchestrated this through prison ministries, decided he would help with the ministry. Bobby gave Joseph the hardware store so he could be free to do other things. Joseph had learned a lot from Bobby and the store flourished. He employed many young men and women while they went to college and many came to a knowledge of salvation while they worked there.

The Institute of Business, where Devon worked, expanded from a junior college to a full college and Devon was promoted to the head of the department. He was kept very busy there but loved his History classes and was able to continue teaching two of those every semester. He and Bobby continued with prison ministries and saw a few souls saved through it.

Thomas and his wife, Carla eventually were placed in charge of her father's business and served the Lord there and in their church.

Angela and I decided to volunteer at the local pregnancy center where I had received so much love and help. There we were able to tell young mothers about Christ's love for them as well as teaching them life skills and helping with their infant's needs.

Ruthie continued classes, encouraged by Anna, and graduated at the top of her class in literature. She found a position nearby and was able to continue living with Bobby until she announced one day she had met a young man and had fallen in love. He knew her story and was as loving to her as Devon was to me. She eventually married and started a family which added to our ever growing family circle.

My brother Bobby started studying Theology, and eventually was called to be the pastor of the church he attended. Anna, Angela, and I decided to home school our children and we met together twice a week to share the teaching.

Mom and Grandma continued to live together for many years, enjoying the kid's visits when Angela and I were volunteering. They continued to have good health and stay relatively independent for many years. Anna was always ready to step in and do whatever was necessary for their happiness and loved having them nearby.

My dad remained in prison but spent his days helping the other prisoners when he could. He encouraged many to come to prison ministry, and God blessed the work. Bobby bought a house which he dedicated to helping those prisoners who were bring released from prison and had no home. He saw a few of them come to know the Lord.

This is the end of the book but by no means the end of God's story. He continues to work in the lives of people everywhere. He has his own people and although they get tangled in a world of sin he guides them through the web. He loves his children. He loved them when he sent his only begotten son to die on a cruel Roman cross as a substitute for them, so their sins would be blotted out and they would be able to live with him in Heaven forever. He loves them now. If you have not come to that place where you realized you were a sinner and in need of salvation, then my dear friend, think on these things. Read God's word, the Bible, find a bible-believing church, and find your friends among God's people. Don't expect them to be perfect. They are all sinners just like you with many failings, but they have been redeemed because God loved them. There can be no real happiness apart from that which is found in him. The riches of this world are useless when the end of your life is near. Our life here on earth is but a season and everyone needs to consider where they will spend eternity. The choice is Heaven or Hell. Hell means eternal torment while Heaven promises eternal joy.

I am grateful that you have read my book, but it would give me greater joy if you were to prayerfully consider the following verses.

All scripture references here and in *Lillian* are from the King James version of the Bible.

Wherefore, as by one man sin entered into the world, and death by sin; so death passed upon all men, for that all have sinned. (Romans 5:12)

For all have sinned and come short of the glory of God. (Romans 3:23)

The wages of sin is death, but the gift of God is eternal life, through Jesus Christ, our Lord. (Romams 6:23)

According as He hath chosen us in Him before the foundation of the world, that we should be holy and without blame before Him in love. (Ephesians 1:4)

But we are bound to give thanks always to God for you, brethren, beloved of the Lord, because God, hath from the beginning chosen you to salvation, through the sanctification of the Spirit and the belief of the truth. (2 Thessalonians 2:13)

All that the Father giveth me shall come to me, and him that cometh to me I will in no wise cast out. (John 6:37)

And hereby we do know that we know him, if we keep His commandments. (1 John2:3)

We know that we have passed from death unto life, because we love the brethren. (1 John 3:14)

Not forsaking the assembling of ourselves together, as the manner of some is; but exhorting one another, and so much the more, as ye see the day approaching. (Hebrews 10:35)

If you would like more information please write to lammey13@aol.com

About the author

Jean McDowell started writing after she retired from her nursing career. She was born in Northern Ireland and married her pastor sweetheart Jim. Jean followed him from country to country, congregation to congregation, and then from state to state in America. They now live in Duncan, Oklahoma. The Lord has led Jean to give all income from this book to Charis Pregnancy Help Center, where she was a volunteer.

Printed in the United States
by Baker & Taylor Publisher Services